Gently Touch Sheela Jenkins

Hilda Stahl

Cover Illustration by Ed French

bethel publishing
1819 S. Main, Elkhart, IN 46516

Dedicated with great love to
T.L. and DAISY OSBORN
for helping to heal the
scores of broken hearts

Chapter 1

is hand brushed hers as he took the letter she had just finished typing and her stomach knotted painfully. She stepped back, only to collide with her desk. He felt her tension and looked up, his fine brow cocked, his green eyes puzzled.

"Aren't you happy with the letter, Sheela?"

She cleared her throat. "I believe I said what you wanted, Aaron." He was her boss and she wanted to call him Mr. Brooks, but he wouldn't permit it. After working together three years, he had said that he was tired of formality. Sheela had consented but she didn't like his casual manner. It was hard to keep up the barrier so carefully erected against him, against everyone.

As he read the letter, she heard someone walk past the door. Pushing a wisp of hair off her cheek, she glanced at Aaron then quickly away to watch rain spot the window. Nervously she fingered a rubber band in the pocket of her suit.

He bent over her desk and scribbled his signature with the gold Cross pen that he carried in his inner jacket pocket. He felt her draw into herself. Did every man make her this nervous or was it him in particular? He slid the letter across the desk and tucked the pen away.

"Send it out today, please. I think that will assure us the account with Chow Down Dog Food." His green eyes twinkled as he pushed back his dark gray jacket and stood with his hand resting lightly on his lean hip. Aaron watched for a smile from her, hoping to see her wide mouth turn up and her blue-gray eyes sparkle. But she only took the letter and carefully folded it into an envelope. Disappointment rose inside him. After three years of cold reserve, he wanted to see what really made Sheela Jenkins tick. She was a top secretary, but she never got personally involved and that bothered him more than he cared to admit.

Sheela could feel him watching and her nerves tingled. She forced her hands to stay steady as she sealed and stamped the envelope. Why was he suddenly taking such a close interest in her? Would he ask her again about her personal life? Had she frozen him sufficiently the last time he asked so that he wouldn't overstep the bounds again? She didn't want him to know that she was often lonely and that she never went out with anyone.

Carefully she filed the carbon copy of the letter away, her hands icy. Why didn't he go back to his own office? She wasn't worth bothering with. She had nothing to offer him. She wanted to be a business machine, nothing more.

Aaron studied her thoughtfully, taking in her navy blue suit and white blouse with no frills. She was attractive even though she tried to appear plain. She was too young to be so unhappy, so uptight. Her shoulder length dark hair looked soft and smelled clean. Occasionally he caught a whiff of perfume, but she seldom wore any. Why wouldn't she be friendly to him? Did she suspect him of immoral motives? She knew that he was a Christian. Maybe she thought because he had a special woman friend it wouldn't be right.

Why couldn't he pull aside Sheela's hard shell and look at the real woman beneath? Maybe then he could think of other things and not find himself returning to thinking of her the minute his business was over.

Nervously she picked up the green watering can and watered the plants hanging around the window. Fall rain splashed harder against the window and she suddenly remembered she had left her umbrella beside the refrigerator at home. Maybe the rain would stop before she had to walk the few blocks to her apartment.

Finally she turned to face him and lifted her chin, almost defiantly. "Did you want something more, Aaron?"

He rattled the change and keys in his pockets. "No, Sheela. I suppose I don't want to go back to my office and listen to the rain beat against the windows. I'm afraid fall is not my favorite time of year." He wanted her to ask what his favorite time was, but he knew she wouldn't. "I like spring and summer. How about you?"

She had no favorite season. Weather didn't matter one way or another to her. She shrugged, then rolled a clean white sheet of paper into the typewriter. She did have several letters to answer but they weren't urgent and she knew they could wait until he finished talking, but he was putting her on edge. She lined a yellow pencil up with her stapler, then dropped a rubber band inside her desk drawer.

Aaron knew what she was doing and he frowned, puzzled even more, then his eyes twinkled. Somehow he would get through to her. He turned a straight backed chair around and straddled it, resting his arms across the back. She looked up, startled, as he hid a mischievous grin behind his hand. "Let's talk about the TV ad for Momma Rosa's Spaghetti Sauce. Have you seen it?"

Sheela nodded as she folded her hands in her lap. She couldn't tell him that she stopped everything just to watch all of his TV ads. "I like it and the company is pleased, I'm sure."

"I know sales have increased. I wonder if we should come up with a cartoon-type ad. Maybe make an Italian Green Giant and Sprout." He chuckled, then sat very still as he watched a smile start in her eyes and slowly move to her lips. What could he say to make her laugh aloud? In the three years she had worked for him, he could count on one hand the times she'd laughed aloud. Today he had to hear her laugh. The intensity of his feelings surprised him.

Just then the door opened and a short, heavy man walked in. He stood just inside the door, twisting a soiled cap in his hands, staring intently at Sheela. He was dressed in dark green twill pants with matching shirt. Rain spots covered his thick shoulders. The smell of cigar smoke drifted from him.

Sheela gasped and locked her cold hands together.

Aaron pushed himself up, studying the man, then looked questioningly at Sheela. Her face had become as white as the stack of paper on her desk. Aaron stiffened, then slowly turned back to the man. "Could I help you? I'm Aaron Brooks."

The man didn't take his eyes off Sheela. "I got to see Sheela." He took a step toward her and she stifled a cry. "Sheela, I got to talk to you." His face was red and his breathing ragged as if he'd been running.

"You shouldn't have come here," snapped Sheela, frowning. She felt Aaron's questions and trembled.

"I had to come, Sheela. It's Bobby."

Aaron hesitated. He knew he should leave, but he couldn't walk away if Sheela needed him. He saw the strain on Sheela's face and felt her tension. He wanted to reach out to her, but he knew she wouldn't accept his hand.

Sheela licked her suddenly dry lips. What was her mother up to this time? "What about Bobby?" she asked coldly.

Color drained from the man's face. He gasped and clutched at the chair that Aaron had vacated.

"Careful!" Aaron stepped forward. "Here. Sit down, sir." Aaron eased the man down, then turned to Sheela. "He needs a glass of water. Would you get it, Sheela?"

She hesitated. Would her legs hold her long enough to walk to the restroom? It would be terrible if she collapsed in front of Aaron.

The man moaned and pressed an unsteady hand to his heart.

Aaron loosened the man's collar. "Sheela, better hurry."

She forced herself up and walked to the bathroom. Weakly she leaned against the counter, her head down while the water ran until she knew it was cold. She filled a paper cup, then walked back to the office, the water sloshing almost over the rim.

Aaron took the cup from her and she stood beside him while he helped the man drink.

She cleared her throat. "Aaron, this is my mother's friend, Wade Grochowalksi."

Aaron shot a look at her. He thought her mother was dead.

Wade wiped a beefy hand across his mouth. "You got to go to Bobby, Sheela." He sounded desperate. "She needs you. She's been in a . . ." His voice broke and he leaned back, gasping and sniffing. "She's been in an accident and she's hurt bad."

Sheela clutched at the nearest object. Her hand closed over Aaron's arm. "Is she going to . . . to die?" Her voice sounded far away. If she wasn't careful she'd faint.

Wade shook his head. "No. But she wants you." He jammed his cap on his balding head and carefully pushed himself up. "I better get back. You want a lift?"

"No."

"You can't walk to the hospital and I know you won't catch a cab or bus."

"I'll take her," said Aaron.

Sheela gasped, lifting startled eyes to his. "No! I'm not going." She turned back to Wade. "You've been taking care of Bobby for almost two years now. You go to her. I have work to do." She wanted to release Aaron's arm, but knew if she did, she'd collapse.

Aaron laid his hand over hers, startled at the icy feel of it. He felt her jerk and he immediately moved his hand. "You can take the rest of the day off, Sheela. Go with Wade to see your mother. She needs you now." He knew how he would feel if his mother were hurt and in the hospital. Nothing would keep him away.

Slowly, carefully, she walked to her chair and sat down. A cold knot tightened in her stomach. Her jaw was set in a stubborn line. "Wade, you go to

Bobby. I have work to do."

Wade moved from one foot to the other. "Don't be like this, Sheela."

She eyed him coldly, but didn't speak.

"She needs you."

Aaron cleared his throat, but didn't speak.

"I'm not going, Wade." Sheela's voice was strong and firm. Inside she was quivering. If Wade didn't leave soon she'd shatter into a million pieces in front of him and Aaron.

Wade sighed loud and long. "I didn't think it'd work."

Sheela frowned.

Wade tugged on his jacket. "Bobby's not hurt."

"What?" cried Aaron.

Sheela's brows shot up. "Is this another trick of hers?"

Wade swallowed hard and finally nodded.

"You tell her nothing will persuade me to see her, Wade. Nothing!"

Aaron fingered his tie. "What's going on here?"

Wade shrugged and walked out, closing the door with a bang. Music drifted in from another office in the building. Rain lashed at the window.

Aaron rested his hands on Sheela's desk and leaned down toward her, a puzzled expression on his face. "Sheela, what's going on here?"

She squared her shoulders. "If you don't mind, I don't want to discuss it further." Her voice was cold with a sharp edge to it and she saw him draw away slightly. Her heart jerked. "You have more important things to do than think about me or my mother. I'll be fine and so will Bobby."

"And how do you know?"

"I know. Believe me. I know." She adjusted the paper in the typewriter.

He knew she'd dismissed him and frustration surged through him. Why wouldn't she accept his help? She was certainly different from his sisters. They loved his attention and his help. He buttoned one button on his jacket. "Sheela, take the rest of the day off. I think you should go see your mother. I know I can't force you, but I can do my part by sending you out of here."

She looked down at the yellow pencil on her desk, her heart thudding until she thought he could hear it. Why should he care what she did or didn't do outside this office? What could she say to make him realize that she'd be better off here in the security of the office, working to keep her mind occupied? If he knew the truth he'd understand and leave her alone, but she dare not tell him the truth.

Aaron stepped back from her desk. "Sheela, you are going!" He carefully set the chair in place, then stood beside it, waiting, watching Sheela's expressionless face. What was she thinking? Why didn't she want to go to her mother? He stabbed his long sensitive fingers through his thick blond hair, then jerked at the knot of his black tie.

She darted a look at him and knew that she couldn't talk him out of her leaving. Slowly she stood. Her legs didn't collapse, so she walked to the small closet and lifted out her all-weather coat. Before she could slip into it, he took it from her. Her heart raced in alarm. She could not survive if he touched her. He held the beige coat and she very carefully slipped her arms into the sleeves. He settled it on her shoulders and she froze, but he immediately stepped back and she relaxed. She was only a few inches shorter than he, but he seemed to tower over her.

"I'll be back in the morning," she said around the

tight lump in her throat.

"Fine." He opened the door into the carpeted hall, then frowned. It was still raining and he knew she walked home. "Where is your umbrella?"

She buttoned the last button on her coat. "I forgot it." She walked past him, but as she reached to open the outside door he said, "Wait, I'll drive you."

She closed her eyes, her hand frozen to the door handle. Rain splashed on the cars parked along the street. She turned determinedly. "I want to walk. I want to be alone."

He grinned at her. "Just as soon as I drop you off you can be alone." He held her gaze for an eternity, then strode toward her, pushing his arms into his coat.

Sheela walked across the carpet to the glass door and stepped out into the cold rain. Ducking her head she walked away from the tall brick building. She bit the inside of her full bottom lip, then walked with him to the silver Cadillac at the side of the building. He opened the passenger door and she slipped in. The warmth surrounded her. The smell of leather and a faint aroma that belonged only to Aaron were irritatingly pleasant.

He chuckled softly, one hand on the wheel, one on the key. "Now is this so bad?"

Sheela glanced at him and almost smiled. "I guess not."

"I don't know where you live."

She told him reluctantly and he frowned, knowing that it wasn't the kind of place that he wanted for her.

"Do you live with someone?"

"No. Alone." She clasped her purse against her and sat rigidly as he backed out of his spot and drove quietly onto the busy street. People scurried along the sidewalks, some with umbrellas, some without. A dog huddled against the front of a drug store, looking wet and cold. Sheela looked quickly away.

"My mom still likes to think I live at home even though I'm almost thirty years old. She wants me to find the right woman and get married."

Sheela shot him a look. "Mariette Golden?"

Aaron chuckled. "Do you think she's right for me?"

Sheela shrugged. "How would I know?"

"Remember the Cootie Catchers we made in school? Maybe that's how I should find out if Mariette's the one."

"That's terrible!"

Aaron stopped at a red light. "It is, isn't it? No. I have a better way."

"Oh?"

"I've prayed. The Lord will help me to know."

Sheela glanced out her window. Aaron had a personal relationship with God that she envied.

"Now that I'll soon be thirty and my business is going well I think it's time to think seriously about marriage." He slowed for a blue Honda to turn in front of him. "What about you, Sheela? Do you plan on marrying?"

She gripped her purse tighter. "I don't think about it." Sometimes late at night when she couldn't sleep she'd wonder how it would be to have a husband who loved her, and then she'd remember her mother. "No, I don't want to get married."

"Don't you want a family? Children?"

"No." The word was a mere whisper and it hurt her throat.

"You'll change your mind. You're young. Not quite fifty. Right?"

She tried to smile at his joke but her face was frozen. She glanced up just as he drove past her apartment. "Let me out here."

He slowed, then shook his head. "I wasn't watching the numbers. I'll turn around. I don't want you walking in this cold rain."

"I've walked in it many other times, Aaron." She sounded impatient and snapped her mouth closed. She was grateful for the ride, and for his thoughtfulness.

He pulled into a driveway, waited until traffic cleared, then backed out and drove back to her apartment building. It was a large gray building that wasn't quite slum, but was far from gracious living. He parked across the street. "I hope you can patch things up with your mother."

She opened the door and rain whipped against her leg. "Thanks for the ride."

"See you tomorrow." He wanted to walk her to her door, but he sat still and watched her run lightly up the walk to her front door.

She fumbled with her key, frantic that he'd follow her and see her place. She looked over her slender shoulder to find him still in his car watching her. He lifted a hand in a wave. Suddenly he looked very lonely and for a split second she wanted to reach out to him to take away his loneliness.

She turned the key, pushed open the heavy door and stepped inside the warm hallway. She leaned weakly against the door, then finally forced her legs to carry her up the flight of stairs to her small apartment.

Smells of coffee and rolls drifted through the dimly lit hall. A TV blared from old Mrs. Ketchum's room next door and the noise increased as Mrs. Ketchum poked out her white head. Her blue eyes snapped wider.

"Sheela! Home so soon?"

Sheela ducked her head and slipped the key in the lock. "Just for today, Mrs. Ketchum." Today she had no patience for anyone, not even for gentle Mrs. Ketchum.

"Are you sick, dear?"

Sheela shook her head and stepped inside her apartment. She pushed the door shut with a loud click and turned the dead bolt lock with trembling fingers. Slowly she walked across the shabby carpet to the faded blue chair that the last occupant had left. She shrugged out of her damp coat and let it fall in a heap near a mystery that she'd been reading. Sounds of Mrs. Ketchum's TV drifted through the wall along with the smell of fresh coffee.

With a low moan Sheela sank into the chair, wrapped her arms around herself and tried to stop shivering. The room was warm but the chill came from deep inside her and she shivered harder. Her eyes were haunted and her face a sickly gray.

"Oh Bobby!"

Sheela closed her eyes and pressed her lips into a thin, tight line. She would not, could not, go to Bobby, not now, not ever.

Chapter 2

he was ten years old.

She tugged a strand of short dark hair over her face and tried to hide the bruise as she walked into Ms. Wilson's fourth grade. Sheela glanced nervously at Ms. Wilson but she was busy talking to Mr. Beck. Sheela sat at her desk and locked her icy hands together in her lap. She watched Jane walk in with Sue and Tonya, but they didn't speak to her and she was glad. Ms. Wilson already paid enough attention to her to make up for ten people. She'd get even more suspicious if Mr. Beck told her that she wouldn't play in gym two days of last week.

Sheela's stomach tightened into a cold, hard knot and she pressed back against her seat. Why didn't Mr. Beck just leave the room? It was time for school to begin. The bell had rung already. What was he saying to Ms. Wilson?

Finally Mr. Beck walked out and Sheela breathed

a sigh of relief. The morning dragged until it was recess. Slowly Sheela walked outdoors while the others raced to see who could get out first. She stood near the back door and watched Jane and Tonya playing soccer. Sue ran to the swing with two other girls. Wind blew tattered papers across the sidewalk. A truck drove past.

Sheela sighed and pulled her pink jacket closer around her. Where was Mike? He was her friend, her only friend in all of fourth grade, in all the world. Finally she saw Mike facing the bully of the room. Fred was tall and fat and made Mike look very small. Fred looked like he was ready to punch Mike. Sheela's anger rose and she ran to Mike's side. She jabbed the air with her fists and danced around the boys. "Hit him like this, Mike! Don't run away from Fred. He's nothing but a big bully!"

"Shut up, Sheela!" cried Fred, his round face red. A wide black belt held his jeans up around his middle. "You get away from here or I'll make you swallow your teeth!"

"You and who else?" She looked quickly around to see if Ms. Wilson was nearby just in case Fred did try to hit her. Ms. Wilson was across the playground with her back to them. Sheela snapped her mouth closed and stepped closer to Mike. She didn't want Fred to hit her. It would hurt too much. But she didn't want him to hurt her only friend either.

"I'm not going to fight you, Fred," said Mike with a firm shake of his head. He pushed his hands into his jacket pockets and looked steadily at Fred.

"You're scared, that's why!" Fred stepped closer. "I'll get you alone some day and you won't get away from me." He turned and ran toward a group of boys near the track.

Sheela breathed a deep sigh, then glared at Mike.

"Why don't you stop him from picking on you? You don't have to be scared of that big bully."

Mike tugged his brown jacket over his jeans. He pushed his sandy hair back. "I am scared of him. He's too big for me to fight."

Sheela shook her finger under Mike's nose. "Don't say that! Don't ever say that again! If you let him pick on you, he'll always do it. Stand up to him and fight." She wanted to shake Mike hard and make him do what she said. She didn't want him to let anyone push him around. It was terrible to be pushed around and be beat all the time.

Abruptly she turned away and ran to the monkey bars. Shouts and laughter filled the air. The steel bars felt cold to her hands as she climbed to the top and peered down at Mike below. He looked small. Everyone looked small from where she sat. Even Momma would.

Sheela shivered and bit the inside of her lower lip. She must remember to call Momma, Bobby.

"Call me Bobby from now on, Sheela," Momma had said a few days ago as they stood in the middle of her tiny living room. "I saw this girl on TV today. Her name is Barbara just like mine and she has everyone call her Bobby." Momma had tugged her yellow sweater down over her jeans and smiled. "I look like a Bobby, don't you think?"

Sheela had nodded. It was very important to remember everything that Momma said. She had to remember to call her Bobby. It wasn't easy to remember, but she would. She'd make herself remember!

She hadn't heard Mike climb up beside her until he said, "What's wrong, Sheela?"

"Nothing's wrong." Oh, if only he knew, but she couldn't tell him. She couldn't tell anyone.

"You're shivering. Are you cold? Or are you as

scared of Fred as I am?"

"I am not afraid of Fred."

"Do you know what Fred did to Chad Peters? He sat right down on him and cracked his rib."

Sheela touched her ribs. Already this year she'd had four cracked ribs. She knew how Chad felt.

"I wish we were both bigger," said Mike with a sigh.

"Me too! Then nobody could beat us up. We would be strong enough to protect ourselves. Or big enough to live on our own."

Mike looked at her with a strange expression on his face and she quickly scurried down the monkey bars and dropped to the soft dirt, but he followed and dropped beside her.

"Who beat you up, Sheela?" he asked with a puzzled frown.

She stood very still. Oh, he dare not learn the truth! "That's a dumb thing to ask me, Mike. Who would beat me up?"

"I don't know. What about that bruise?"

She covered her cheek. "I fell and hit myself on the side of the couch."

"Oh."

"Don't you believe me?"

He shrugged. "I guess."

She turned away and walked slowly to the slide. Her legs felt weak and shaky. Had Mike guessed? She was glad when he ran off to join Tommy.

Someday she'd be big and strong and she'd move far, far away from Bobby. She'd never see or talk to Bobby again.

After school Sheela walked home with Mike the way she did each day since Bobby had been hired at Burger King. They talked about soccer and their library books. She stopped outside the back door. It was getting harder and harder to be around Mike's mother. She asked too many questions about the bruises. Sheela was running out of answers.

She picked a needle off the evergreen bush beside the back door. "Mike, I think I'll just stay outdoors and play while you change."

"Don't you want milk and cookies?"

Her stomach growled with hunger, but she shook her head. Finally he shrugged. She watched him walk inside and heard his mother greet him as if she was glad to see him.

A few minutes later Mrs. Lowber stepped outdoors and smiled at Sheela. "How are you today?"

Sheela stiffened. What'd she mean by that? Sheela tried to hide the bruise on her cheek. "Just fine, Mrs. Lowber."

"What happened here?" Mrs. Lowber touched the bruise gently and Sheela jerked back.

"I fell down!"

Mrs. Lowber fingered the tiny gold butterfly on the chain at her throat. "Honey, I'm your friend. I love you. If you ever need help, call me. I'll help you. I will. I've told you to come to me if you have a problem."

"I don't have any problems," Sheela said quickly, too quickly. "I never have problems." She crossed her fingers behind her back and stood very, very still. Finally Mrs. Lowber changed the subject to school.

Much later Sheela walked down the street to the tiny gold house where she lived alone with Bobby. Bobby's blue car stood in the drive. The neighbor's gray cat ambled across the small grassy front yard. Buds hung on the lone maple tree.

Sheela closed the front door as quietly as she could, then stood with her back pressed against it. The smell of fresh fingernail polish sickened her. She swallowed hard, then managed a smile as Momma looked over at her from where she sat on the couch admiring her red nails. "Hi . . . Bobby." She almost called her Momma. "I'm sorry I'm late . . . Bobby."

Bobby shrugged her slender shoulders. Once she'd had brown hair the color of Sheela's but now it was a flaming red and fluffed around her pretty face. She was dressed in a pink robe that touched her delicate ankles as she crossed her shapely legs. "Mrs. Lowber called to say you'd be late." Suddenly she frowned and leaned forward. "You didn't tell her to call so I wouldn't be mad, did you?"

"Oh, no, Bobby! I wouldn't do that." The door knob pressed into her thin back.

Bobby leaned against the couch with a tiny sigh, then touched her forehead with the back of her slender hand. "What a day, Shee. I worked real hard, taking all those orders. I think my back's out of place from carrying trays and cleaning up after all them folks."

"I'm sorry," said Sheela barely above a whisper.

Bobby fluffed her hair. Her nails were painted the same shade of red as her hair. "Did I tell you that I have a date tonight?"

Sheela was able to walk to the chair across from the couch and sit down. Bobby was usually in a good mood when she had a date. "Who with?"

Bobby smoothed her robe over her knees and looked very pleased with herself. "With Duncan. I met him when I got gas today. He manages that little station on the corner of Bond and Washington. You know the one."

Sheela didn't, but she nodded. It was always safer to keep Bobby talking about herself and the man in her life.

"How was your day, Shee?" Bobby smiled and Sheela shrank back against the chair. She knew

Bobby wouldn't want to hear anything bad.

"It was just fine. I did good in reading."

"I told you you would if you tried harder." Bobby shook her finger at Sheela. "You listen to me, and you'll get better grades all the time. My momma made me get good grades." Bobby's face darkened and she fingered the small scar beside her right ear, and Sheela shivered. "I'm not like Momma, Shee. I say you should do the best you can even if it doesn't mean getting top marks all the time."

Bobby dropped her hand back in her lap and Sheela relaxed slightly. She knew why Bobby touched the scar each time she talked about her mother. In a fit of anger Grandma had cut her with a small knife, leaving a scar that had stayed with her all of her growing up years. Sheela didn't like to look at it and she knew Bobby hated it.

The roar of a motorcycle broke the silence and Bobby leaped up and ran to the window. She held back the dusty flowered drape and looked out. "It wasn't Pete. I thought maybe he'd stop to give me a ride again, but I guess his wife won't let him." She flipped her hair back and lifted her chin. "Who needs Pete? I got Duncan now and he's not married." She walked to the middle of the small room. "Sheela, open a can of chicken noodle soup for us. I'll shower and dress." Bobby clasped her hands and laughed. "Oh, this is going to be my lucky night. I can feel it."

Sheela waited until the bathroom door closed after Bobby, then she pushed herself up and walked to the tiny kitchen.

Just as the soup was heated almost to boiling, but not boiled or Bobby would be angry, Bobby walked out of the bathroom still in her robe. She smelled clean and looked fresh. The makeup enhanced her wide blue eyes.

"The soup smells delicious. I get tired of smelling hamburgers all day long."

Sheela spooned the soup into two bowls and set them carefully beside a pack of crackers on the table.

Bobby sank onto a chair and tugged her robe over her legs. She reached for her spoon just as the phone rang. She laughed under her breath as she ran to answer it. She curled up in the corner of the couch, her feet tucked under her as she talked.

Sheela crumbled crackers in her soup, then dipped in her spoon. She liked the way the crackers turned from thin and crisp to fat and soggy. The first bite was too hot and she quickly sipped her icy water.

"What do you mean? You said you'd be here!" Bobby's voice was sharp with anger and Sheela stopped eating to stare in alarm at her. "How can you say that?"

The spoon dropped from Sheela's fingers and clattered to the table. Desperately she looked around. Could she make it to the door before Bobby could catch her? A bitter taste filled her mouth and she slowly stood.

"Don't make any more excuses, Duncan. Just tell me you don't want to go with me." Bobby's voice rose and Sheela cringed back, trembling with terror.

Slowly Sheela walked from the kitchen to the living room. The door seemed miles away. She glanced at Bobby and saw her flushed cheeks and snapping blue eyes. Sheela reached for the door knob with a trembling hand. Bobby slammed down the receiver and cried, "Sheela Jenkins, don't you dare take another step!"

A band tightened around Sheela's thin chest and she slowly turned to face an angry Bobby. Then Bobby shrugged.

"Don't look so scared, Sheela. I'm not like

Momma. I'm not going to beat you just because Duncan broke our date. Who needs him? He's not worth even that!" She snapped her fingers, then flipped back her flaming hair. "Come on back to the table and we'll eat our supper."

Sheela crept across the floor and sat at the table. How could she eat? Slowly she picked up her spoon. The lump in her throat was too large to allow anything to pass it.

Bobby took a sip of soup, then frowned down at it. She took a bigger sip and frowned harder. "Cold! Cold!" She pitched her spoon across the table and it hit the wall right next to the clock. The spoon fell to the floor with a clatter and Sheela froze, her eyes wide and her heart racing.

"Do you really expect me to eat cold soup after working hard all day long? What an ungrateful girl you are! How dare you feed me cold soup?"

Sheela's hand trembled as she reached for the bowl. "I'll . . . warm it . . . for you."

"Cold soup!"

Sheela lifted the bowl, but her fingers refused to hold it and it dropped from her hand, spilling across the table and dripping down on Bobby's lap.

Bobby leaped up with a shriek. "Now, look what you did! You'll be very sorry for this, Sheela Jenkins!"

"No!"

"I know you did that on purpose. You hate me. Just like everyone does!"

Sheela raced for the bathroom to lock herself in until Bobby's anger passed, but Bobby grabbed her arm and spun her around, sending her flying to the floor. Before Sheela could move Bobby picked up her curling iron and lashed out with its cord. Pain exploded across Sheela and she cried out, but no one heard her and no one came to help.

Chapter 3

he leaped from her chair, her heart pounding. It had been a long time since she'd remembered in such vivid detail Bobby's terrible beatings.

"Wade did it." Sheela's voice tore through her tight throat. "He brought back . . . the . . ."

She shook her head. "No! I won't remember! I won't think about it another second!" She tore off her suit, hung it carefully in her minuscule closet, then pulled on jeans and a dark blue sweater. She brushed her hair away from her pale face with short, jerky movements. Her soft brunette hair hung down to her shoulders in a cascade of waves. Lillian Ketchum's coffee aroma still hung in the air. Water rushed through the pipes and made them rattle. Someone walked past her door whistling and she knew it was By Windfield. He and Mrs. Ketchum played gin rummy every afternoon. Mrs. Ketchum had given her that piece of news one day when they met in the laundry room. Sheela had tried to stay to herself, but Mrs. Ketchum was too talkative to freeze out and Sheela didn't have the heart to hurt the woman's feelings by telling her outright to leave her alone.

Sheela glanced at her watch and frowned. It was already five o'clock. Soon it would be dark and she had a few groceries to buy. The store was only two blocks away, but she hated walking after dark.

Rain no longer hit against the window. The sky was gray and bleak. "It suits my life," she muttered as she pulled on her jacket.

A few minutes later she walked into the brightly lit store, dropped her purse in a cart and walked slowly down the first aisle. The predominant smell was a pine cleaner that a man was using as he scrubbed the floor with a string mop. Another customer stood near the produce and someone was checking out. Music played over the sound of the beep of the cash register and the chatter of two boys near the comic book rack. Sheela dropped a box of tissues and a pack of paper towels in her cart. In the produce section she found lettuce at a price that offended her, two tomatoes, two cucumbers, and a small pack of carrots. She hesitated at the frozen chicken, then picked up a box along with frozen vegetables. She glanced up to see a man, woman, and two children shopping together, talking and laughing. Was that what a real family was like? Outside of TV was there really a real family? Sheela bit her lower lip and hurried down the aisle away from them.

What would it feel like to belong to a family? How would it feel to sit at a table to eat together? Several times when she was in fourth grade she had shared a meal with Mike and his family, but that was before she had moved away, leaving her totally without friends.

Impatiently she tossed a loaf of wheat bread into her cart next to her purse. She pushed her cart around the end of aisle 9, then stared in shock. Bobby and Wade were walking into the store. Bobby's bright red curls lined her carefully made up face and hung to her slender shoulders. She wore a pink and white jacket over pink slacks. Her high heeled black shoes tapped lightly on the floor as she walked beside Wade, talking in her usual high-pitched chatter. Bobby looked much younger than her years and she didn't seem unhappy at all the way she claimed to be. Sheela's legs trembled and she clung to the cart. They dare not see her! She couldn't handle another confrontation today. She whirled around and rushed out of sight of the front door. Her cart bumped into the front of another cart with a loud clatter and she stopped dead, breathing unevenly as she stared at the woman on the other side of the cart.

"Hey, it's okay," said the woman with a laugh.

"Sorry," whispered Sheela. She started to back away.

"Hey, don't I know you?"

Sheela frowned. The woman was tall and slender with dyed blond hair held up and back from her slender face with a thick green clip that matched the green in her multicolored jacket. Her brown eyes were warm and friendly looking.

She wagged a long, slender finger with bright red polish on the nail at Sheela. "Sure. Sure, I do. You live in the same building as me. I'm Jill Konikof. Apartment 5. Me and my little girl Addie live there."

"Oh. Oh, yes. I've seen you with Mrs. Ketchum." Sheela darted a look around. Bobby and Wade weren't in sight.

"Hey, are you all right?"

Sheela pulled herself together enough to nod.

"I'm ready to check out. How about you? Hey, maybe we can go home together. I'd offer you a ride, but I walked. Did you walk?"

"Walk?"

"I think you're really out of it, aren't you?" Jill touched Sheela's shoulder, then wrapped her long fingers around Sheela's arm. "Hey. What's going on with you? You're as white as that roll of paper towels."

Sheela took a deep breath. "Nothing's wrong with me. Really. You just go ahead." She pulled back until finally Jill's hand fell away. "I can manage on my own."

Jill shrugged. "If you say so."

Trembling, Sheela rolled the cart to the check out. Maybe she should leave her cart and run home without her groceries.

"Sheela! Wait!"

It was Bobby. Stiffly Sheela turned. A bitter taste rose in her throat.

Bobby ran to her and reached out for her, but Sheela cringed back. Bobby let her hand fall to her side. Her face puckered as if she'd burst into a loud wail at any minute. "I need to talk to you, Shee. Don't be mad at me."

Sheela lifted her chin slightly and said in a low icy voice, "We have nothing to say."

Bobby's blue eyes filled with tears. "Come on, Sheela. You can't keep this up. I need you. You need me. We're family."

Sheela shook her head. "No. We aren't. I'm leaving. You find Wade and be a family with him."

"I miss you."

"Tell that to someone who will believe it."

"Let's go have coffee together."

Sheela's legs trembled, but she didn't let Bobby see. "No. I told you that I won't see you or talk to you. Ever. I meant it."

Bobby opened her mouth, then snapped it closed. Slowly she turned and walked to Wade who stood silently waiting near the magazine rack.

Sheela forced her mind away from Bobby and paid for her groceries without peeking to see if Bobby was still standing nearby watching her. She rushed out of the store into the chilly fall evening. Weakly she leaned against the brick siding and took several deep breaths.

"Hey, Sheela, are you all right?"

She spun around to find Jill looking in concern at her. "I . . . I'm fine."

"You don't look it. You look ready to fall flat. Can I help you?"

Sheela shook her head, then glanced apprehensively toward the door to see if Bobby was walking out. She wasn't, but Sheela couldn't relax.

"Hey, can I help you?"

"No. No, I'm all right."

"Hey, I guess we can walk together after all." Jill grinned and hiked up her bag of groceries.

Sheela didn't have the energy to disagree. She gripped her bag against her thudding heart and waited for another shout from Bobby. None came and Sheela breathed easier. She fell into step beside Jill.

"Where do you work, Sheela? I'd like to get to know you. I think we're the same age and all. You don't mind me asking you things about yourself, do you?"

Sheela glanced at Jill, barely hearing what she said.

Jill took it for assent.

"I work at the Copper Door on Lark Street. You a waitress, too?"

"No."

"A cook?"

"Secretary."

"Secretary? Don't they pay you enough to live better?"

Sheela only shrugged and walked faster.

"Hey, if I could afford a better place I'd get me and Addie out of there fast. But I do have Mrs. Ketchum to watch Addie and she does it real cheap." Jill carefully stepped over a bad crack in the sidewalk. "You gotta watch out for them cracks." She was silent for several steps. "You ever play that game, step on a crack, break your momma's back?"

"I guess."

"I did. Sometimes I'd step on the cracks on purpose." Jill sucked in air and giggled nervously. "You think that's mean, don't you? I bet you had a nice momma and a happy home."

Sheela's knuckles ached from gripping her purse. "We'd better hurry or we might get caught in more rain."

"It is starting to blow some. I would've driven to the store, but my car's in the shop again. Who knows what's wrong this time. Every time I turn around that car breaks down. You got a car? I never see you drive one."

"I don't have one."

"How come?"

"I don't need one."

"Ever have one?"

"When I first moved here, but it broke down too many times and I got rid of it."

"Maybe that's what I should do. But it'd tie me

down too much. Don't you feel tied down?"

"No."

Jill was silent for several minutes. They started up the walk toward the front of their apartment. "Hey, it's been nice talking to you, Sheela. Let's get together for a cup of tea or something, shall we?"

"I don't know. I'm pretty busy usually."

"Yah, me too. But, hey, we're only young once, you know. I used to tell Greg that. He's my ex. He got too tired to do anything, but watch football on TV."

Sheela fumbled in her purse for her key. Youth wasn't what TV showed it to be and it didn't bother her to grow old and die and be done with a life that really wasn't worth living anyway.

"Here, I'll unlock it for you. My arms aren't as full as yours." Jill pushed her key in and opened the heavy door. "I'm beat tonight. I hope Addie's not in one of her moods."

Sheela had caught glimpses of ten-year-old Addie when she was leaving Lillian Ketchum's apartment. Addie seemed very quiet and unsmiling. Sheela walked toward the stairs with Jill beside her. At her door she said, "Goodbye. I hope you get rested."

"Me too. Addie better be quiet tonight." Jill tilted her head. "You ever hear her screaming?"

"No."

Jill nodded. "Good thing. I don't want her upsetting anyone."

"Goodbye," Sheela said again as she opened her door. She stepped inside and breathed a sigh of relief.

She put away her groceries without allowing herself even a tiny thought about Bobby, mechanically fixed a quick dinner and ate in silence, then jumped up and ran to the TV. It was time for Channel 8

About Town with Aaron's commercials.

Smiling slightly she watched the furniture store ad that came on at two of the program breaks. Aaron was glad when Marlett Furniture asked him to handle their advertising. He shared his excitement with her, but she'd hurt him by not responding. She bit her bottom lip and groaned. "I can't care for him. I won't," she whispered as she clicked off the TV. "I won't be hurt ever again."

At seven-thirty someone knocked on her door. She gripped the sponge tighter as she turned from washing off the top shelf of the refrigerator where she'd spilled pickle juice. Could it be Bobby? Sheela shook her head and took a deep breath.

"Don't do this to yourself. It won't be her. It's probably Mrs. Ketchum."

With a frown Sheela dried her hands and slowly walked toward the door, expecting to find Lillian Ketchum from next door, but instead Jill stood there with Addie. Addie wore faded pink pajamas covered with tiny yellow kittens and carried a hardcover book. She looked ready to cry.

Jill tugged her black jacket closed over her red sweater. A bright red clip held a clump of blonde hair high over her right ear. Tight jeans covered her long, slender legs. "Hey, Sheela, I need a favor. I wouldn't ordinarily ask you, but since we got to be kind of friends a while ago, I thought I'd ask."

Sheela tipped her head and puckered a brow. "What?"

"I have to go out tonight just to clear my head and all." Jill stepped away from Addie. "Mrs. Ketchum can't watch Addie, and I was wondering . . . Could you keep her here with you? I mean, just for a while. Hey, I'll understand if you don't want to, but I got to get out or I'll go crazy."

Sheela glanced down at Addie as Addie looked at her mom with a frightened look on her face. Something about the look on Addie's face tugged at Sheela's heart. "I don't think Addie would feel comfortable with me since she doesn't know me."

"That won't bother Addie." Jill nudged Addie's shoulder. "Will it?"

Addie ducked her head. "No."

Sheela wanted to refuse, but she found herself saying yes instead and opened the door wider for Addie to enter. "If you're sure you won't be afraid, Addie."

"She won't be. Hey, I'll be back about ten, I think. You really did save my life here, you know."

Sheela nodded.

Addie walked across the room without looking back.

"Hey, see you later then." Jill's face lit up as she turned and ran toward the stairs, her high heeled red boots clicking loudly.

Sheela slowly closed the door. The smell of pickle juice drifted up from her hands. What in the world would she do with Addie until ten o'clock?

"You won't have to worry about me," said Addie, as if she'd read Sheela's mind. "I brought my book to read."

Sheela managed a smile. "What is it?"

"It's called 'Shadrack's Crossing' by Avi." She held up the blue hard cover book with the picture of two boys dressed in overalls walking in water.

"Is it good?"

"It's very exciting." Addie walked to the couch and sat in the corner and opened her book.

Slowly Sheela sank in her chair, watched Addie a while, and finally picked up her book. She read, conscious of Addie nearby. From time to time Sheela glanced at Addie. She was engrossed in her book and Sheela let her read. About nine o'clock Sheela started to ask if Addie wanted something to snack on only to find Addie's head bobbing in sleep.

Sheela pulled a blanket off the foot of her bed and after a moment's hesitation carefully slid Addie down until she was lying on the couch. Sheela covered her and let her sleep. She looked at peace, making Sheela realize how tense Addie usually looked. With a shrug Sheela walked to the kitchen and drank a glass of water and finished washing the refrigerator shelf. Having Addie in her apartment took the edge off the loneliness that she'd accepted as part of her life.

She rubbed lotion on her hands, smelling the light scent. Water rushed through the pipes again, making them rattle.

Suddenly Addie shrieked and sat bolt upright, her eyes wide in terror and her face a sickly gray.

Fear pricked Sheela's skin as she ran to the couch and dropped down beside Addie and caught her hands. "What's the matter, Addie?"

Addie trembled violently and tugged her hands free. She cringed against the corner of the couch.

"It's all right, Addie. Remember? I'm Sheela Jenkins and I'm taking care of you while your mom's out."

Addie looked around and finally turned wide eyes on Sheela. "I guess I just had a bad dream."

"I'm so sorry. Are you all right now? Can I get you something?"

"I'm all right." Addie huddled into the corner of the couch and pulled the blanket over her.

"Want to tell me about your bad dream?"

Addie shook her head hard. A wisp of her tangled light brown hair hung over a dark eye and she pushed it back with an unsteady thin hand.

Sheela scooted back and sat with her arm across the back of the couch and her right knee bent as she faced Addie. "Dreams aren't real, you know. Dreams can't hurt you."

"I know," whispered Addie. She rubbed the back of her hand across her nose. Some of the color had returned to her cheeks. "Sometimes it seems real."

"I know. I remember." Sheela didn't know what else to say. She wasn't used to being around children.

Addie twisted the edge of the blanket around her delicate finger. "Did you sometimes have bad dreams when you were a little girl?"

"Yes. Sometimes."

"About what?"

Mostly about Bobby, but Sheela couldn't tell Addie that, so she just shrugged and forced back her own anguish. "That was a long time ago."

Addie sighed heavily. "I dream bad dreams lots of times."

"I'm sorry."

Addie glanced around again. "What time is it?"

"About nine-thirty."

"I guess she'll be back soon."

"Your mother?"

"Yes. She said about ten."

"But she sometimes comes back late. That's why Mrs. Ketchum doesn't like to watch me at night. She comes in late and Mrs. Ketchum wants to get her sleep because she's old and needs her rest."

"If she comes back late you can sleep right there and I'll sleep on my bed. I'll wake up when she knocks."

"Wouldn't you be mad at her for being late?"

Sheela shrugged.

"I would be. I wouldn't want to be stuck with some little girl that I don't even know."

Sheela smiled gently. "I don't mind. Sometimes I get tired of being alone." She'd never admitted that aloud to another person.

Addie smiled and her brown eyes lit up. "I don't mind being alone."

"I don't either."

Addie looked down at the blanket over her knees. "She went out with Jack. She thinks it's funny." Addie glanced at Sheela. "Jack and Jill."

Shella laughed. "I guess it is funny."

"I don't like him."

"Why not?"

"He's mean to her."

Sheela didn't want to get into that subject. "What grade are you in?"

"Fourth."

"Do you like school?"

"I guess." Addie hooked her hair behind her ears. "Did you when you were my age?"

She didn't, but she didn't want to say that. "It was all right."

"I'm good in reading. I read a lot. You like to read, don't you?"

"Yes."

"Mom can't read as good as I can."

"Oh?"

"Sometimes I have to read things for her. It makes her mad." Addie shivered and frowned, then pulled into herself. "I think I'll read again."

"Or maybe you should lie down and sleep again."

Addie yawned. "I might."

"Do you want a glass of milk first?"

"I guess so."

"Come to the table and I'll give you one. How

about a cookie? I have a few sugar cookies left that Mrs. Ketchum gave me." Sheela smiled over her shoulder as she walked toward her tiny table.

"Thanks. I like her cookies." Addie hiked up her pajama bottoms and tugged down her top. "Sometimes I help her make them. She's nice. Sometimes I pretend she's my grandma." Addie sat on one of the chairs and Sheela the other.

Sheela handed two cookies to Addie and she kept two. She asked more about the book Addie was reading and listened as Addie told her in great detail.

Someone knocked at the door and Addie's words died in her throat. "That's her."

Sheela ran to the door and opened it wide for Jill. "We're having cookies and milk. Would you like some?"

Jill frowned around Sheela at Addie. "She knows she can't eat this time of night. Get yourself over here, little girl, and let's go."

The haunted look returned to Addie's eyes as she dashed to get her book and join Jill.

Sheela felt the tension between mother and daughter and it alarmed her. "Don't blame Addie, Jill. I asked her to have cookies and milk with me."

"Well, she knows better." Jill shoved Addie ahead of her out the door. "This has been a rotten night. Thanks for watching the brat for me."

"You're welcome. Good night, Addie. I'll see you again."

Addie nodded.

"I bet you never have a bad time with a guy, do you?"

Sheela only lifted a fine brow. Jill didn't need to know that she never went out.

"I thought he'd be fun. Jack, I mean. Jack and Jill.

Get it?" Jill tried to smile, but looked ready to cry instead. "But, hey, what can I expect from a loser?"

"Maybe tomorrow will be better." Sheela touched the door.

"Ha!" Jill patted back a yawn with the tips of her fingers. "Tomorrow's never any better even when I think it's going to be."

Addie moved from one slippered foot to the other.

"Can't you stand still one little minute while I say a polite good night?"

"Sorry," whispered Addie against her chest.

"Good night," said Sheela.

"Good night." Jill poked Addie's back. "Let's go. Do you think we can stand here all night?"

Addie dashed off with Jill trailing behind her.

Slowly Sheela shut the door and leaned against it. She didn't like what she was thinking. "No. No, it can't be. She's just impatient. She's not going to . . . to hurt Addie."

But Sheela stood at her door and listened for a long time. If Addie cried out in pain she didn't hear her.

Chapter 4

heela gripped her black umbrella tighter with both hands as she stepped away from the protection of her apartment building. A gray bag that held her purse, shoes, and lunch hung around her neck and down the side of her back. Black boots kept her feet warm and dry. Wind caught at the umbrella and tugged and she tipped it forward to keep it from turning inside out. Icy rain whipped against the parts of her that the umbrella didn't protect. A siren wailed in the distance. She saw a man's dark, shiny shoes and legs from the knees down covered with dark slacks stop at her side.

Aaron caught her arm and she gasped and jerked, but he wouldn't release her. He smiled into her startled face. "I didn't want you walking in the rain."

Seeing him there almost took her breath away and caught her totally off guard. A black raincoat covered his dark suit. "But . . . but I always walk."

"Not anymore now that I realize it." He grinned and his green eyes twinkled. "My car's right there. It's warm and dry inside. Come on." She finally walked with him to his car and slid in as he closed her umbrella and pushed it on the floor of the back seat. Just seeing her brightened the day for him and he ran around to the driver's side to slip under the steering wheel. "Isn't this a beautiful day, Sheela?"

An unexpected smile turned up her pink lips and her blue-gray eyes sparkled. "What are you talking about? It's terrible out."

He laughed. He hadn't felt this good in a long, long time. Yesterday when he'd left her he'd gone back to the office feeling sad and lonely. It had been hard to keep busy even with Don talking to him about the Buddy Account. "Let's go on a picnic. What do you say?"

She chuckled and shook her head. The sound of her laughter touched his heart like nothing he'd experienced before and he wanted to hang on to the moment.

"We have work to do today, Aaron. Even on such a sunny, beautiful day."

"We'll call the boss and tell him we have more important things to do."

"He might fire us." Deep inside she knew she shouldn't be playing games with him, but she couldn't stop. He'd caught her totally off guard and she couldn't drop her icy cloak back in place.

"Not us! We're too important to the company." Aaron looked back to make sure the way was clear, then he pulled onto the street. The car tires hummed quietly on the wet pavement. The heater blew out comfortably warm air. "Besides, I have an in with the boss."

"But I don't."

"Sure you do. He'd never fire you. You're too important to him." He had started out in a bantering voice, but ended up sounding very serious. The words hung between them and he wanted to look at her to see her expression, but he couldn't take his eyes off the rush hour traffic around him.

She couldn't look at him, but turned to stare out the side window. Just then he drove past his office. She tensed. "Where are you going?" Suddenly the shield dropped around her and she pulled into herself. "Let me out right now." Her voice was colder than the rain.

He stopped at a red light and turned to her with a disarming smile. "Don't be frightened."

"Frightened?" Her voice rose and she swallowed hard. "I'm not frightened. I don't want to go anywhere with you."

He grinned. "Do I look dangerous, Sheela Jenkins? Would I harm you?" He wanted to kick himself for moving too fast for her. She was afraid of him and he would have to deal with that carefully. "I'm sorry. I was going to stop for breakfast and I thought maybe you'd want to also. But if you'd rather not, I'll take you back to the office immediately."

"Breakfast?" After last night she had overslept and hadn't eaten this morning. She was hungry. "I suppose that would be all right."

"How about the Copper Door?"

"Fine." She shrugged and tried to smile, but couldn't.

"I've eaten there before and the food's good."

"A woman in my building works there."

"What's her name? Maybe I know her." At the green light he drove forward, then pulled into the parking area of the Copper Door.

"Jill Konikof. She has blond hair and is tall and talks a lot."

Aaron nodded. "Yes, I've seen her in there. Quite a friendly woman."

"Very," Sheela said drily.

Several minutes later Sheela sat at the oak booth with padded seats across from Aaron. Condiments and a plastic advertisement of desserts stood just under the window. Country music played in the background, but she could still hear Aaron as he talked to her. She'd ordered a bacon omelet with a cup of tea. He had asked for two fried eggs, hash browns, whole wheat toast and a glass of milk.

"It doesn't look like Jill is here," said Sheela, glancing around the small restaurant. Three other booths held people and several men lined the counter. Smells of hot cakes, coffee, and bacon made Sheela's stomach ache with hunger.

"Are you friends with this Jill?" He found he had to know about her life outside the office.

Sheela shrugged. "Not really. I babysat with her little girl last night. Addie."

This was the first conversation he'd ever had with her outside of work subjects. He enjoyed it. "How old is she?"

"Ten."

"I have a ten-year-old cousin. Brian. He's never quiet."

"Addie likes to read. She's very quiet. I think . . . I think . . . Never mind."

He leaned forward. "What?"

She'd almost told him her suspicions about Jill beating Addie, but she couldn't say it aloud. "Never mind. It was nothing." She looked away to see the blond waitress bringing their order. "Oh, here comes our breakfast."

Aaron moved the napkin that he'd balled up and dropped in front of him. "Smells good."

Sheela waited until the waitress left before she laid her napkin across her lap. "It does smell good."

"Is it all right with you if I bless our food?"

She stiffened. It hadn't occurred to her. "Sure."

He bowed his head and softly prayed, "Father, thank you for your great love to us. Thank you for this food. Bless Sheela this day. In Jesus' Name, Amen." He lifted his head and smiled right into her eyes.

Flustered, she picked up her fork and cut off a piece of omelet.

"They make real hash browns here." Aaron lifted a bite to his mouth. "Most places grate cardboard and fry it in margarine. But here they use real potatoes."

A laugh burst out of her before she knew it was coming. He enjoyed the sound of it more than the taste of the crispy hash brown. She ducked her head and ate in silence. His feelings toward her confused him and he tried to sort them out as he ate. It was very strange that suddenly she was important to him as a woman. Before, he'd cared about her because she worked for him, because she was an excellent secretary and he wanted to keep her happy so that she'd stay. But now he wanted to know all about her. He wanted her to care about him, not just as her employer, but as a friend.

She sipped her tea and tried to find a way back to her isolated island where she belonged. How had she allowed him to intrude into her private life?

He dabbed his mouth with his napkin. "My mother's coming in today."

"Oh?"

"She has an appointment with the dentist and she wanted to visit me." He smiled. "She's a great lady."

She listened as he went on and on about his mother. He did the same when he talked about his dad, his brother and his two sisters. She had briefly met them all, but had kept them at arm's length even though they'd all been very friendly.

"Sheela, tell me about your mother."

Sheela choked on the swallow of tea.

"Are you all right?" He reached over and lifted her hands up high as if she were a baby. She stopped choking immediately and tugged away from him.

She flushed painfully. "Don't you think we should get back, Aaron?"

He pushed up his white cuff and looked at his gold watch. "I suppose we should. I told Don we might be late, but we'd better get back before he thinks he can take over the business."

"He would make a good partner for you."

"I've been thinking about it. He knows advertising and he has brought in his share of business. I guess I'm not ready to share my business with someone else."

"It would give you time for more of a personal life." Now, why had she said that?

He nodded. "That's true."

"Mariette Golden will like that." She wanted to grab back the words, but it was too late.

He frowned and motioned for the check. He liked Mariette, but he wasn't considering marriage and neither was she. It upset him to have Sheela think differently. "Mariette and I are only good friends, Sheela."

Sheela's heart leaped and she ducked her head in confusion. Why should she be glad to hear that statement? "Ridiculous," she muttered under her breath as she slipped out of the booth to get her coat.

Several minutes later she sat at her desk and

answered the phone as it rang. She transferred the call to Aaron, then rolled a paper into her typewriter.

"So, did you have a hearty breakfast, Sheela?"

She glanced up to find Don Clark standing across from the desk. New jeans covered his long thin legs and a red and black sweater hung loosely on his muscular chest. His light brown hair was combed back neatly. "An omelet and tea. How about you?" She smiled. She liked Don. He never tried to get past her reserve. He'd have treated anyone who sat at her desk the same. He was married to a pretty girl named Roxie and they were expecting a baby before Christmas.

"Granola. Roxie made it. She says it's good for the baby." He laughed and his dark eyes crinkled at the corners. "You like granola?"

"I've never had it."

"It's good. Especially with nuts and chocolate chips in it." Don glanced over his shoulder. "Aaron busy?"

She saw the red light showing on the phone. "He's talking to a client."

"I'll wait." He sank to the corner of her desk. "Waiting, waiting. Do you ever want kids, Sheela?"

She froze. "No."

"I'm beginning to think I don't either. Roxie has two months before the baby and she just sits and stares at a calendar, waiting for the days to go. She says she can't wait to hold the baby in her arms. She's tired of waiting. So am I."

"The light is off. Aaron's free now."

"Good. Talk to you later." He strode across the room and walked into Aaron's office.

Sheela leaned back and closed her eyes. Would she want a baby? Tears burned her eyes. She dare not think about it. She would never take a chance on treating her child the way Bobby had treated her and Grandma had been with Bobby.

"Are you all right, Sheela?"

She jerked forward to find Aaron's mother standing across from the desk. "Mrs. Brooks, I didn't hear you come in."

"That doesn't matter, Sheela. Are you in pain?"

"No." She jumped up. "Would you like to sit down until Aaron's free?"

"I've been to the dentist and so I'd rather stand for a while." She flipped off her black coat and Sheela quickly took it and hung it in the closet beside hers.

".I could get you a cup of coffee, Mrs. Brooks."

"That would be nice."

"Don is with Aaron right now. I'll let Aaron know you're here." Sheela buzzed Aaron and when he answered she said, "Your mother's here."

"Thanks. Tell her I'll be right out."

Mrs. Brooks leaned close to Sheela and said into the phone, "Don't hurry, Aaron. I'll visit with Sheela."

Sheela smiled stiffly as she hung up. Slowly she looked up at Mrs. Brooks. She looked younger than her fifty years with her hair colored a light brown and her body still youthful and slender. "I'll get you that coffee."

"Thanks. And I'll have a chair now." She set the chair near the desk and sat down crossing her slender legs. She wore navy blue hose with her navy suit and red silk blouse. Several strands of silver chains hung down on her blouse and matched the silver clips on her ears.

Sheela hunted for something to say. It was hard to be around Mrs. Brooks. She was nothing like Bobby and Sheela couldn't relate to her as a mother.

"Aaron tells me you walk to work."

Sheela moved restlessly. "Yes."

"I'd like to offer my car to you to use."

"Oh, my, no!"

"I insist. I can use Tera's Dodge. She left it with me since she bought a new one."

Sheela could only shake her head. "I really don't mind walking. It isn't far."

"I know, but what if you want to go across town? Or out of town?"

"I won't."

"At least consider it, Sheela."

"Thank you. But, really, I don't need a car."

She hadn't heard Aaron's door open and didn't realize he was in her office until he said, "Turned you down, Mom? Save your breath. Sheela can be very, very stubborn." Aaron smiled as he leaned down and kissed his mother's cheek.

"Hello, Nola," said Don. He stepped around Aaron and kissed her other cheek. "It's good to see you."

"You, too, Don. How's Roxie?"

"Impatient."

Mrs. Brooks laughed. "I can remember how that feels."

"Only two months."

Mrs. Brooks patted Don's arm. "I'm planning a baby shower for her next month. That should help."

"She'll like that."

Sheela watched and listened and suddenly felt left out of life. She looked down at her hands locked in her lap and struggled against her depression.

"See you later, Nola." Don kissed her again and strode to his office.

"Come to my office, Mom," said Aaron. "I want to hear about your great trip to the dentist."

"No cavities," she said and laughed as she

walked with Aaron. She turned at the door and smiled at Sheela. "Talk to you later, Sheela. And I'll have Aaron deliver the car at your doorstep."

Aaron laughed and winked at Sheela, then ushered his mother into his office.

Sheela stared after them, shaking her head. Why were they so set on helping her when she didn't want help?

In his office Aaron hugged his mother to him. "I like your perfume."

"Thanks. You bought it for me for my last birthday."

"I did?" He laughed as he stepped back from her. "I have good taste."

"Yes, you do." She touched his cheek and smiled. Her blue eyes lit up with love. "I'm glad I could see you today. I missed you Sunday."

"I missed you, too."

She sat on the soft chair near his desk and looked up at him. "Now, suppose you tell me what you have in mind for Sheela?"

He tilted his head and leaned back against his desk. "I don't have anything in mind. She needs help and I intend to see that she gets it."

"And is that all it is?"

"What do you mean?"

She shook her finger at him and laughed. "You know what I mean."

He lifted a fine brow. "Mom, I wish I knew. There's something about her that touches me."

"Oh? She's been with you three years. Why now?"

"I don't know." Slowly he walked to his leather couch and sat down, then leaned forward, his forearms on his legs. "I just know I want to see the haunted look leave her eyes. I want to hear her laugh more than twice a year. I want to hear her chatter about her life the way Priscilla and Tera do."

Mrs. Brooks pushed a strand of hair off her smooth cheek. "Obviously she was raised differently than your sisters."

"What happened to make her the way she is?"

"Aaron, are you beginning to fall in love with Sheela Jenkins?"

He jerked up. "In love?"

"You spend a lot of time with her. She's distant, but she is sweet. You can't hide the truth from yourself."

"But, I'm not falling in love with her, Mother!" He tugged at his tie. "At least I don't think I am. I never thought about that."

"Maybe I shouldn't have said anything. You're a kind person and you want the best for others. That might be what you're feeling toward Sheela."

"Yes . . . Yes, it might be." He stabbed unsteady fingers through his blond hair. "I hope I haven't given Sheela the wrong impression."

"She's a very sensible girl."

"You're right. I don't have to worry about that. It's just that if she thinks I'm interested in her with love in mind she'll run and hide and I'll never see her again." With the grace of a panther he stood and walked to his mother. "You do understand, don't you?"

She stood and slipped her arms around him. "I do understand, but it really doesn't matter if I do or don't. Sheela is the one who must understand your actions."

He rested his cheek on his mother's head. "I'll keep my distance so that I won't frighten her away. But I will continue to try to help her."

"I'm glad. I'll do all I can."

He stepped back and leaned against his desk.

"Mom, I've told her often that God loves her, but I know she doesn't believe it. I'll continue to pray that her spiritual eyes be opened to God's truth. She needs to know that God really loves her, really wants to be a part of her life."

"Yes, she does, Son."

"Mom, Mom, sometimes I want to hold her close and protect her from anything harmful."

Mrs. Brooks pulled Aaron's face down and kissed his suntanned cheek. "Aaron, you're going to make some girl a fine husband."

He flushed. "Mom, don't jump to any conclusions."

She looked very innocent. "Did I do that?"

"Mom," he said in a warning voice. "You've been after me for almost five years to get married. I thought you agreed to stop talking about it."

She smiled. "Did I?"

He laughed and hugged her. "You did, and I'm holding you to your word." He walked around his desk and sat down. "Now, tell me how Dad's doing. I've seen him on TV every afternoon, but it's been about two weeks since I talked to him." With difficulty he pushed thoughts of Sheela away and listened to his mother.

Chapter 5

istlessly Sheela dried her plate and set it in the cupboard. The evening stretched long and lonely before her. Wind whistled around the apartment building and blew cold rain against her front window. Heat trickled from the floor heater and took off the chill in the room. She rubbed a hand over the sleeve of her blue sweater. Faded jeans hugged her slender legs and warm blue socks kept her feet from freezing. She wiped the towel across the counter and then stood looking unseeingly across the small room. Just before five while Aaron was on the phone she'd slipped away from the office before he could force his mother's car on her. She would not accept anything that would put her in debt to anyone. The walk home had been wet and cold, but no different from many other times when she had walked, except that she constantly looked over her shoulder, expecting to see Aaron following her.

Just then someone knocked and she jumped and dropped the dishtowel. She scooped it up and flopped it over the edge of the white sink. Her heart raced as she forced herself to walk to the door. "Who is it?"

"It's me, dear. Lillian Ketchum. With Addie."

Sheela sighed in relief and opened the door. "Hello." Lillian Ketchum wore a plaid wool coat over dark slacks and a beige sweater. Her white hair waved back off her lined face. From the look in her bright blue eyes Sheela knew something was troubling her. Addie stood quietly, wearing jeans, a pink sweatshirt, and grubby white tennis shoes.

Mrs. Ketchum nudged Addie ahead of her. "Can we come in?"

Without a word Sheela stepped aside.

"I need you to take care of Addie." Mrs. Ketchum gripped her black purse tighter. "Jill was supposed to be back fifteen minutes ago so I could go visit a friend. And she's not back."

Sheela looked helplessly from Mrs. Ketchum to Addie. "I don't know."

Addie hooked her hair behind her ears. "She's going out with Jack again. But I can stay by myself. I can. I'm big enough."

"No." Lillian Ketchum shook her head. "No." She glanced pleadingly up at Sheela. "Sheela?"

She shrugged and nodded. Another puff of wind rattled the window. "I'll watch her."

Mrs. Ketchum smiled and patted Sheela's arm. "Thanks, dear. I didn't know if you would, but I thought I'd ask. Addie said you watched her last night. I'll stop in when I get back in a couple of hours and if Addie's still here I'll take her."

Addie frowned and crossed her thin arms over her thin chest. "I won't be here."

"Don't worry about it," said Sheela. "Addie will be all right with me." She glanced at Addie and saw the bruise on her pale cheek, and her knees trembled, but she managed to smile at Addie. "She can stay here until her mother comes."

Mrs. Ketchum buttoned her plaid coat. "Oh, I'm glad! I was so counting on seeing Wilma tonight. I could've taken little Addie with me, but Wilma has this thing about children."

"You go visit your friend and have fun."

"I will. I'll leave a note for Jill on my door. See you later, Addie."

"Bye."

Sheela closed the door after Mrs. Ketchum. "She's a nice lady."

Addie nodded, her dark eyes serious.

Sheela noticed the bruise again, but couldn't bring herself to ask about it. "Did you eat?"

"Yes. With Mrs. Ketchum. Soup and crackers."

"I have some leftover salad if you'd like some."

Addie squared her thin shoulders. "You don't have to feed me."

"I know. Would you like some salad? It's very good. I put cheese and bits of chicken in it."

Addie narrowed her eyes in thought and finally nodded. "But I can get it myself."

"It's right in the refrigerator. There's dressing on the door. Take what you want." Three bottles of dressing sat on the door next to mustard and catsup. "And here's a bowl."

"Thanks." Addie fixed her salad while Sheela boiled water for a cup of tea.

Sheela reached for another cup. "Want tea?"

"I guess. With lots of milk and sugar."

Sheela made a face, but fixed the tea with half milk and a full teaspoon of sugar. She set it beside Addie, then sat down in the other chair. "How was school today?"

Addie chewed a bite, swallowed and finally said, "I didn't go."

"Oh?"

Addie touched the bruise on her cheek, then jerked her hand away as if she'd burned her finger. "I didn't feel very good this morning."

"Is that right?" Sheela tensed. "A cold?"

"No. Just didn't feel like going." Addie filled her mouth with lettuce and a slice of tomato.

Sheela sipped her tea. She couldn't handle getting involved if Jill indeed was beating Addie. "My boss Aaron Brooks and I ate breakfast at the Copper Door this morning." Just saying Aaron's name sent a tingle through her.

Addie lifted up her cup and gulped her tea. "Mom didn't go to work until ten-thirty."

"I noticed she wasn't there."

"She worked until five and then she had a date." Addie frowned as she leaned an elbow on the table and propped her chin in her hand. "She said she wouldn't go with Jack again even if Jack and Jill was cute, but she went so she wouldn't be bored staying home."

Sheela glanced at the rain. Wind rattled the window casing.

Just then someone knocked and Sheela jumped. "Maybe that's your mom."

"I doubt it." Addie jumped up and faced the door with her fists clenched at her sides and her back stiff.

Sheela opened the door to find Zelda Bracie, the manager of the apartment, standing there. Zelda's perfume rushed at Sheela, choking her.

"You know I'm not a messenger, Sheela Jenkins!" Zelda folded her slender arms over her full breasts and glared. Bright red curls bounced around her head and hung down on her shoulders and back. Her orange jumpsuit fit so tight Sheela wondered how she could walk in it.

"Hello, Zelda."

She insisted everyone call her by her first name, her stage name. She told everyone who listened about her five years in New York. She said she was taking time off acting to get her strength back so that she could go back fighting and make it to the top. She stamped her slippered foot. "Sheela, there's a man on the phone downstairs for you. I said I wouldn't get you, but he insisted."

Sheela froze. "Who is it?" If it was Wade she would refuse to take the call.

"Aaron Brooks."

Sheela's heart fluttered. "Oh."

"He said he will speak to you now." Zelda tightened the wide belt at her slender waist. "He's insistent. You get down there right now and answer it and you tell him not to call you here again. Got it?"

Sheela nodded. "Go tell him that I'll talk to him at work tomorrow."

Zelda shook her head so hard her curls flipped all over. "No way, no way! That man is used to getting his own way. You talk to him, and I mean it, Sheela."

Sheela turned to Addie. "Will you be all right alone for a few minutes?"

"Yes."

"Are you sure?"

"She's not a baby," snapped Zelda.

"I'm not," whispered Addie.

"All right, but lock the door, Addie. I won't be long." Sheela slipped on her shoes, stuffed her keys in her pocket and walked down behind Zelda whose high heeled slippers tap-tapped on each step.

Suddenly Zelda stopped and sniffed. "I know I smell a cat." She glared at Sheela as if she had the cat up under her sweater. "When I find out who's keeping a cat in my building I'll kick him or her out. Do you know who has a cat in here?" Zelda fluttered her hands and wrinkled her nose, the most predominant part of her face. "Oh, never mind! You wouldn't tell me anyway!"

Sheela didn't say anything as Zelda continued down the stairs in front of her. She knew Byron Windfield had a big white cat named Nadia, but Zelda was correct; she'd never tell.

"Pets aren't allowed and everyone knows it. One of these days I'll find out who has it and fur will fly. Fur will fly." She stopped, thought a moment and giggled. "Fur. Cat fur will fly."

Sheela turned away with a groan and with a trembling hand picked up the receiver that Zelda had dropped on the shelf under the wall phone. "Hello, Aaron." Her voice was strong, never giving away her tension.

He leaned forward over his desk. "Sheela, you didn't take the car."

"I know."

"I'm going to deliver it in just a few minutes. I'd wait until tomorrow, but I must go out of town early tomorrow until Tuesday."

"I didn't know."

He wanted to ask if she'd miss him, but he didn't dare. "It came up suddenly. Don will handle everything at the office."

"I'm sure he'll do well."

"Will you be all right?"

"Yes." She twisted the phone cord. "But I won't take the car."

He leaned back with a frown. "Sheela, it's already settled."

She gripped the receiver tighter. "I won't take it."

"It'll be there . . ." He glanced at his watch. "At seven. Be sure you unlock the door for me or I'll have to anger your landlady. You wouldn't want that." He chuckled and she forced back a smile.

"I won't drive it."

"It'll be there for you."

She sighed heavily. "Won't you change your mind?"

"No."

"All right. But I won't drive it."

He laughed softly. "See you at seven."

"See you." Slowly Sheela hung up the receiver and turned to find Zelda listening. Sheela frowned.

Zelda stepped forward with a scowl marring her well-made-up face. "So, you're getting a car."

Sheela lifted her chin. "Yes."

"You don't have a parking space."

"But my rent covers a place for me."

"I have my RV there. You said you weren't using it and so I do."

Sheela walked toward the steps, stopped at the bottom and said over her shoulder, "You'll have to move your RV."

"I won't." Zelda stamped her foot and shook her head. "And don't you dare think you can make me."

Sheela started to answer, shrugged and walked back upstairs. She wouldn't argue with Zelda. This was a perfect way out. When Aaron came she'd tell him to take the car back because she didn't have a parking space. It really was better that way. She pulled out her apartment key and smiled as she unlocked the door.

Addie had her bowl and fork and tea cups washed

and put away. She ran to the door. "She's mean."

"Zelda?"

"Yes. She thinks she's going to get rid of Nadia."

Sheela's eyes widened. "Do you know about Nadia?"

"Yes, but I promised By I wouldn't tell anyone. He lets me play with her sometimes while I'm with Mrs. Ketchum."

"I told him he'd have to be more careful. " Sheela dropped her keys back in her purse and slipped out of her shoes. "Now, what'll we do?"

Addie walked around the room. "I didn't bring a book. Do you have anything for me to read?"

"I don't think so. All of my books are for adults. I don't have any games either. How about TV? Want to watch? But maybe only news is on."

Addie sat on the couch. "Channel 17 has LITTLE HOUSE on. I like Laura, don't you?"

"Yes. She has a nice family." Sheela flipped the channels until she found 17. "I used to watch it."

Addie hugged a pillow to her. "It's all reruns and I've seen them all lots of times. I sometimes pretend I have a mom and dad like Laura and Mary and Baby Grace."

Sheela saw the yearning on Addie's face and she quickly turned away to watch TV. Against her will her mind flashed to Aaron and his insistence to help her. What had come over him lately? Had he learned about her past and was trying to make up for it with acts of kindness and attention?

No! He dare not learn about her past. It would be too embarrassing and too humiliating.

Just before seven she said, "Addie, I must go downstairs again. I shouldn't be too long, but if I get held up, will you be all right alone?"

Addie nodded. "Don't worry about me. I told you

that I'm not a baby."

Sheela smiled and nodded. "I know. It's just that I don't want you to be nervous here on your own."

"I won't be. I'll watch TV until you get back."

"All right. See you in a little while." Sheela caught up her purse and slipped on her shoes. Lightly she ran downstairs to the empty hall.

She stopped at the door and watched Aaron stride up the sidewalk, his head bare and wind ruffling his blond hair. He wore jeans and a dark green leather jacket. Her heart skipped a beat and she frowned. Quickly she pushed open the heavy door and he stepped inside, bringing in crisp, cold air and a hint of after-shave. The rain had stopped, but puddles stood along the sidewalk.

Aaron smiled and his green eyes twinkled. "Hello," he said softly. Just seeing her sent his pulse leaping.

She stepped back from him. "I'm sorry that you went to all this trouble for nothing, Aaron."

"Don't worry about it." He dangled the key in front of her. "Tell me where to park it."

"There is no spot." She knew she sounded triumphant, but she couldn't help it.

"No spot?"

Quickly she told him about Zelda taking her spot. He frowned. "Isn't a parking space in your lease?"

"Yes."

"Then you have a space. Let's talk to this Zelda."

"Oh, please, no!" Sheela caught at his arm, then at the warm contact she dropped her hand to her side. "I don't want any trouble."

"I won't bite her. I just want to set this whole thing straight." He glanced around, found the sign that said MANAGER and walked purposefully toward the door.

Sheela plucked at his arm. "Aaron, I don't want the car."

"I will not go out of town until I know you have it."

"But I haven't had a car for two years."

"And I didn't know it, but now I do, and I can take care of it." He rapped on the door and Sheela hung back, her face white. How she hated a confrontation with Zelda! Aaron glanced back at her, smiled and winked and part of the ice around her heart melted.

The door flew open and Zelda stood there, her eyes blazing. They softened at the sight of the handsome man. The TV blared behind her. "Yes?"

Aaron smiled and introduced himself. "I need to park Sheela's car. Tell me where to put it, please."

Zelda stiffened. "I already told her there's no place."

"She told me, but I know and you know that Sheela doesn't like to fight with anyone. But I don't mind. So, where do I park the car?"

Sheela watched Zelda's shoulders slump in defeat.

"Number 10 is empty for a few days. Park it there until I find a spot for my RV." She slammed the door.

Aaron turned and grinned at Sheela. "That's that."

"I guess it is." She shook her head and laughed. "You're a miracle worker."

"That's right." He walked toward the door. "Where's your coat?"

"My coat?"

"It's cold out. You don't want to run out to the car without a coat on."

"I won't be out long."

"But I want to show you the car and maybe have you drive around the block." He wanted to keep her a little longer since he wouldn't see her for a few days that suddenly seemed like an eternity.

"But I can't be gone that long."

He stiffened. "Oh?"

"I'm baby-sitting Addie again."

Relief left him weak. He was afraid she had a man she couldn't leave. "Just come to the car with me and let me show you a few things on it. It won't take long."

She nodded.

He slipped off his jacket and held it for her. She knew it wouldn't do any good to argue, so she pushed her arms in the sleeves where his had been seconds before. The warmth wrapped around her and reached right to her heart. The sleeves hung almost to her fingertips.

"Perfect fit," he said.

She couldn't answer, but walked to the car with him and slipped inside.

"It's an Olds," he said as he started it up and drove around to the parking area. "It's automatic so you don't have to worry about shifting gears." He kept his voice light as he showed her everything that she'd need to know to drive it. He parked in space Number 10 and sat quietly.

She locked her hands over her purse, suddenly tense. "I should get back to Addie."

He nodded. "I'll see you Tuesday." He dropped the keys in her hand and she pushed them into her purse.

Car lights stabbed the darkness of the alley near the parking area, then were gone. Sheela moved uneasily. The smell of the leather seats blended together with Aaron's after-shave, teasing her senses.

"Take your jacket." She started to shrug out of it, but he stopped her with a hand on her shoulder.

"I'll walk you inside and then take it from you."

"We'll use the back door. It's right there." She pointed to a door almost hidden by two evergreen bushes.

He locked the car and walked with her to the back door. He had so many things he wanted to say to her, but kept them unspoken in case he sent her running back into herself. He watched as she unlocked the back door, her hand trembling slightly.

She pushed open the door and glanced back at him. "Thank . . . thank you for going to all of this trouble for me, Aaron."

"It was no trouble at all, Sheela."

She shrugged out of his jacket and handed it to him. He took it and his hand brushed hers, sending a shock through them both.

"See you Tuesday," he whispered.

She nodded, unable to speak.

"Take care of yourself." He strode away and she stood and watched until he was out of sight.

Chapter 6

heela unlocked her door and slipped into her apartment to find Addie sound asleep on the couch with the TV playing quietly. Addie had taken a blanket from the foot of Sheela's bed and curled up under it. Sheela watched her for a long time. A longing to have a child of her own rose inside her, surprising and frightening her.

Abruptly she walked across the room, and as she passed the door, someone knocked. She opened it quickly before Addie awoke. Jill stood there with a wan look on her face. Sheela tried to feel anger toward Jill, but couldn't.

"Addie's asleep," Sheela said quietly. "I hate to disturb her."

"She'll go right back to sleep in her own bed." Jill listlessly pushed a strand of her blond hair off her pale cheek. "I'm ready for bed, too. What a terrible day!"

Pity for Jill moved Sheela. "How about a cup of tea? Or coffee?" The words were out before Sheela knew she was going to say them.

Jill smiled briefly. "Sure. Tea sounds good right now." She stepped in. Sheela took her coat and hung it over the blue chair.

"We'll sit at the table. Let me wait on you for a change." Sheela led the way to the tiny table. As Jill sat down with a weary sigh, Sheela filled the tea-kettle from the faucet.

"I don't get much waiting on, I'll tell you." Jill reclipped the bright blue clip just off the side part of her hair. "Hey, I bet you get just as lonely as me, don't you, Sheela?"

Sheela only shrugged as she sat down. "Do you get lonely?"

"Me? Sure I do."

"I thought you'd have lots of friends."

Jill rolled her eyes. "There are friends and there are friends. I have lots of lonely times."

"I thought you went out a lot."

"I go out, but if the guy don't like me I might as well be alone. Men! Who needs 'em?" Jill bobbed her penciled brows. "Me, that's who. Can't live with 'em and can't live without 'em." She studied her bright nails for a few seconds. "Addie give you any trouble?"

"None at all."

"Hey, that's good." Jill sighed and leaned back. "I sure do wish I was free like you. No kids to answer to. No troubles. Yah, you got it good."

Sheela bit her lower lip. How wrong Jill was!

"It's not that I don't love my kid. I do." Jill picked at her fingernail. "It's just that she's so much responsibility. Sometimes I don't think I can go on day after day, raising her alone. Her dad won't help with her and I don't have family around here. They wouldn't help if they were."

Sheela moved restlessly.

"Hey, I always thought being an adult would solve everything. Now, I wish I was the kid being taken care of. But I was never like other kids." Jill suddenly leaned forward. "What would you say if I told you my mom beat me when I was a kid?"

All the color drained from Sheela's face. "Don't . . . don't tell me. I . . . I can't listen."

"I should've known. Who wants to hear such a terrible thing? You probably wouldn't believe me." Giant tears welled up in Jill's brown eyes. "I've never told that to anyone. I guess I'm too tired to keep my mouth shut tonight." She jumped up and jabbed at her tears. "I'm getting out of here."

"Wait!" Sheela caught Jill's thin wrist. "The water's ready. Have a cup of tea and rest a while."

Jill sniffed and finally nodded. "Hey, what've I got to lose? I wouldn't be able to sleep if I did go home. The minute my back touches the bed my eyes pop wide open. I hear every little sound and I just know somebody's going to sneak in and slit my throat."

"But the doors are locked!"

"I watch TV, you know. It'd be easy enough to pick a lock and, with my luck, mine would be the room they'd come to."

Sheela filled the teapot with boiling water and dropped a bag in it. She set it on the table with cups and sugar. "Do you take milk?"

Jill shook her head. "Just a few grains of sugar to take the bitter taste away." She sighed heavily and played with the bright blue beads hanging down on her flowered sweater. "I guess I worry over everything. I get so uptight at times that I think my head's going to pop right off my shoulders. I know nobody loves me." She dabbed at her eyes with a tissue from her jeans' pocket. "Maybe Addie does since I'm her mom. But nobody else does."

Sheela ran a finger around the rim of her cup. "Maybe you should see somebody. For help."

"You mean like a shrink?"

"Or a . . . minister."

"Hey, I tried that. I didn't get any place at all."

Sheela lifted her cup and barely sipped the tea. Slowly she sat it on the table. "You could . . . pray."

"Pray! You don't think I don't? I pray and I pray, but I never get answers."

"My boss, Aaron Brooks, has told me of many times that he prayed and God answered. It really is incredible."

"Maybe he should pray for me."

"He would."

"Yah? He doesn't even know me." Jill stirred sugar into her tea. "Why should be bother with me?"

"He's different. He takes to heart this business of caring for others. He and his whole family. You might have seen his dad on TV. Taylor Brooks. He has a talk show; 'The Taylor Brooks Show' on Channel 13 every evening at five-thirty."

Jill sipped her tea as Sheela talked in greater detail about the show. She nodded. "I did see him a while back when he was talking about helping the street people. But mostly I'm at work at five-thirty." She leaned forward and studied Sheela. "What kind of help could they give me?"

"I don't know. But maybe they'd teach you how to have your prayers answered." Sheela felt strange talking about it. Only last week she'd almost asked Aaron to help find God for herself, but she'd backed out.

Jill rolled her eyes. "Some of my prayers I

wouldn't want answered. But, hey, I know what you mean. If I ever get to feeling like I need help again, I'll let you know."

"If you need help with Addie, I'd help you."

Jill stiffened. "Why'd you say that? She been telling you things?"

"I didn't mean anything. I know Mrs. Ketchum can't always baby-sit and I want you to know that I'll be glad to do it if I'm free."

Jill relaxed slightly. "Hey, that's nice of you. Well, I guess I could use your help at times. And you remember that if I can ever help you, I will."

"Thank you."

"Hey, I'm sure there's nothing I can do for you, but I'm still willing to be a neighbor." Jill finished her tea and jumped up. "I better get my kid and go home now. I feel a whole lot better than I did. Thanks, Sheela. You're a good friend."

Sheela managed a smile. In her opinion, she and Jill weren't friends but she didn't want to argue about it with Jill. "I'll wake Addie."

"I never saw her go to sleep so early."

"She was probably overtired."

What'd you mean by that?"

"Nothing." Sheela bent down to Addie and shook her gently. "Addie, your mother is here."

Addie opened her eyes and blinked.

"Hey, get up, Addie."

Addie shot up, flushed and frightened. "Mom!"

"Let's go home. Sheela's had enough of both of us." Jill grabbed up her coat and flopped it over her arm. "Let's go."

Sheela smiled at Addie, trying to reassure her. Before she knew what was happening Addie flung her arms around her and hugged her hard. Sheela gasped and finally hugged Addie back. The smell of

Addie's shampoo was pleasant. Tenderness engulfed Sheela and she didn't want to release Addie. "Come again, Addie."

Addie nodded and ran across to the door.

"Thanks, Sheela." Jill smiled. "The talk helped."

"Good. I hope you have a good night's rest."

"Hey, me too! Bye." Jill closed the door with a snap and Sheela pushed the safety latch in place.

The silence surrounded her. Suddenly the wind rattled the window and the refrigerator turned on. With a ragged sigh, Sheela walked to the window and looked down on the parking area below. She saw the front bumper of the dark blue Olds that Aaron had parked in Number 10. "Oh, Aaron."

Slowly she walked across to the kitchen and back again to the window as she replayed Aaron bringing her the car. Suddenly she stopped.

"How did he get home?"

She clamped her hand over her mouth and her eyebrows shot to her hairline. Why hadn't she asked him? How terrible to think that she'd made him walk home and after he'd been so thoughtful of her!

"I'll apologize tomorrow."

She dropped to the edge of her chair. Aaron wouldn't be in tomorrow, and not until Tuesday. "Oh, my."

She shot up out of the chair and walked across the room. "What am I going to do?" She swallowed hard. "Call him?" she whispered.

Before she could stop herself she grabbed her purse and flew out the door and down to the phone. She'd had to call him often enough at home from her office so she knew his number. She slipped in change with a loud TING and dialed quickly. He answered on the second ring and she almost dropped the receiver.

"Aaron." Her voice faltered.

He leaned against his kitchen counter, his heart thudding against his white tee shirt. "Sheela?"

"Yes."

He jerked up and almost knocked his glass of milk over. "Is something wrong?"

"No. I just . . . just realized you had no way home. I'm sorry. I should've offered to drive you, but it didn't occur to me until just now."

He smiled and leaned down again, his head almost against the overhead cupboard. "How nice of you!"

"But too late!" She twisted the cord and moved from one foot to the other.

"Don't worry about it. I walked to the office where I'd left my car and drove home from there."

"But it's so cold out!"

"You walk every day, Sheela Jenkins!"

That silenced her.

"But no longer. You have a car now."

That she wasn't going to drive, but she wouldn't argue now. "I'm sorry you had to walk. I should've offered to drive you."

"Don't worry about it. It's over." He wanted to keep her on the phone. "I didn't mind walking. It's probably pleasant when the weather's nice."

"It is." She leaned against the wall.

"I ran part of the way."

"I sometimes do, too."

He twisted his stocking foot on the floor tile. "I'm sorry I have to leave in the morning before I get a chance to see you."

"But you'll be back Tuesday."

"Monday night late. I'm meeting Ted Thomas in Grant to talk about his lumber business."

"You'll get it."

"Thank you."

She pushed her fingers into her back pocket. "I'll see you Tuesday."

"Tuesday." He wanted to ask if she'd have dinner with him Monday night, but he knew she'd say no. "Take care of yourself, Sheela."

"You, too, Aaron." She bit her bottom lip. "Goodbye."

"See you." Aaron slowly hung up and walked to his kitchen table where he sank down on the nearest chair. "Heavenly Father, take care of Sheela. Help her to know you love her."

Smiling, Sheela ran back to her room and stood in the middle of the floor for a long time.

The next few days dragged along without Aaron in his office but she worked with Don, keeping his mind on work and off Roxie the best she could. During the weekend she took a walk with Addie.

Tuesday morning she dressed carefully in her blue wool suit with her flowered blue silk blouse. The sun shone brightly as she walked to the office, her bag slung over her shoulder. She had not driven the car except to move it to her own parking spot.

In the office Sheela knocked on Aaron's door. There was no answer and she peeked in. He wasn't in and neither was Don. She watered the plants and answered several letters, always listening for Aaron's step.

Don dashed in, looking rumpled and tired. "Is he here yet?"

"No."

"Roxie's not feeling well and I told her I'd get back home as soon as I took care of a couple of things."

"Let me know if I can help."

"Thanks." He strode to his office and closed the door with a snap. Almost immediately he stuck out his head. "Buzz me when he's in."

"I will." She leaned back in her chair and watched the door, then realized what she was doing and straightened her desk. She frowned. Aaron often went away on business and she'd never watched so intently for his return. Maybe it was because he'd been paying so much attention to her lately.

Abruptly she walked to the window and stood watching the passing traffic. The warm sun and wind of the past two days had dried the puddles. Faded red leaves hung tightly to the oak at the side of the building.

"What am I doing?" She rubbed her hand over her skirt and fixed the collar of her jacket. Somehow she'd have to get control of herself. She dare not allow Aaron Brooks to be too important in her life.

The door opened and he walked in. She spun around and drank him in, from the top of his neatly combed blond head to his highly-polished brown shoes. He wore a dark brown suit, crisp, beige shirt with a striped tie. He studied her from the top of her brunette head down to her high heeled blue shoes.

"Hi," she said at last. She couldn't push another word out.

"Hello." He walked toward her, smiling. He wanted to tell her that he'd missed her. "Is Don here?"

"Yes." She smiled.

"Good." Was she smiling because he was back or because Don was in?

"Did you get the account?"

"Yes."

She laughed breathlessly. "I knew you would."

"You did?"

"Yes."

"It's a great account."

"You'll sell a lot of lumber for Ted Thomas."

"You think so, huh?"

She nodded.

He bobbed his eyebrows. "I think so, too." He took a step toward her. "I'm glad to be back."

She moistened her lips with the very tip of her tongue. "You have a few important calls to return."

"I'll get right to them." But he didn't move.

Don's door opened and he stepped out. "Aaron! Good, you're back."

"Oh, I forgot to buzz you," said Sheela, flushing.

"That's all right." Don stabbed his fingers through his dark hair, spiking it up. "Aaron, Roxie's not feeling well. I've finished a few important things and I'm taking a couple of accounts home with me. Call me if you need me back."

"Don't worry about us. Take good care of Roxie." Aaron patted Don's back. "Call if you need to, Papa."

Don rushed out, leaving behind only the music from the hallway. Before Aaron or Sheela could move, the door burst open again and Wade walked in, his round face red and his broad chest rising and falling with each ragged breath.

"Sheela," he gasped, reaching out for her.

She frowned and stumbled back against her desk. "Not again, Wade."

"No more games," said Aaron firmly. He gripped Wade's arm. "You will not upset Sheela again."

"No game." Wade pulled loose and leaned against Sheela's desk. His thick body rose and fell as he tried to catch his breath. A cap covered his balding head. He wore a plaid overcoat over his dark dress pants and striped shirt. "It's Bobby."

"Stop it!" cried Sheela.

Wade looked at her, his eyes haunted. "She drove to the store this morning for some coffee because I forgot it yesterday. A truck rear-ended her and the car spun and struck another car. She didn't have on a seat belt and she's hurt bad. Real bad." A tear slipped down his cheek. "She needs you, Sheela."

Sheela shook her head. "It's another trick. I know it is." Her lips trembled as she walked to her chair and sank down. Helplessly she looked at Aaron.

He gripped Wade's thick arm. "Is this true?"

"Yes. Call the hospital if you don't believe me."

Aaron scooped up Sheela's phone, found the number and dialed.

Sheela held her breath.

"Ask for Barbara Jenkins," said Wade.

Sheela gripped the arms of her chair. Wade was serious! Chills ran down her back. Aaron's voice sounded hollow as he spoke into the phone. Finally he replaced the receiver and took Sheela's icy hand in his.

"She is there and her condition is guarded."

"You have to be there for her, Sheela," cried Wade.

Sheela shook her head and clung to Aaron's hand. "No. No, I won't," she whispered in a strangled voice.

"But you must," said Aaron.

"No."

Wade twisted his cap in his beefy hands. "You can't do this to your own mother, Sheela Jenkins. It ain't right!"

Aaron looked at Wade. "You go back to the hospital. I'll take care of Sheela."

Wade cleared his throat. "You see that she gets there quick."

"I will."

"No," whispered Sheela.

"You can't let her die without you, Sheela." Wade clamped his cap on and walked out.

Aaron knelt at Sheela's side and studied her intently. "Your mother needs you, Sheela."

She shook her head.

"I'll drive you."

Sheela pulled her hand away and shook her head. "I will not go."

"Get your coat." He strode across the room. "I'm taking you."

This time she couldn't let him force his will on her. She stood behind her desk and met his look squarely. "If you persist in trying to take over my life I will quit my job."

"Sheela!"

"I will walk out the door now!" Her voice rang out, but inside her heart was breaking.

He knew she meant it and he could only stare at her. Slowly he walked toward her. "I don't understand you at all."

"There's no need for you to try."

"But your mother?"

"It's my business."

He shook his head. "I don't understand you at all," he repeated.

"I didn't ask you to." She stared icily at him and finally he turned and walked to his office. Weakly she sank to her chair and covered her face with trembling hands.

Chapter 7

The chill of the fall night air followed Sheela into the quiet hospital. She shook her head and frowned. Two days and she gave in to Wade's urging to visit Bobby. He actually dared to invade her apartment by slipping in the outside door when Mrs. Ketchum had walked out.

Sheela glanced over her shoulder. Not only was she here against her will, but she'd driven the dark blue Olds. Jill was right; life wasn't fair.

Sheela clutched her purse tighter as she walked down the long corridor. Nurses bustled past her. A boy sobbed against his mother's leg. Her words of comfort followed Sheela. Smells of medication, antiseptic and coffee merged together in the hall near the elevator, sickening her. Her hand trembled as she jabbed the up button. Chills ran up and down her back as she stepped into the empty elevator. Wade had said that Bobby was in a coma.

But what if she opened her eyes now? Sheela leaned weakly against the silver bar as the elevator shot up. She did not want Bobby to know that she'd visited her. Bobby might take that as an opening to reconcile.

"Why did I come?"

But she knew why. Wade's pleading, Bobby's serious condition, and Aaron's eyes always on her, always begging her to do the right thing.

Sheela closed her eyes and fought against remembering the years with Bobby. Remembering was almost as painful as living it. Seeing Jill and Addie almost daily and suspecting that Jill beat Addie brought back too much of the pain. But she'd decided that seeing Bobby might take away the fear and part of the pain and erase the guilt that Aaron made her feel. Besides, Bobby couldn't harm her now, not when she was in a coma.

The elevator jerked and the doors slid open. Two men walked in and she stepped out, the smell of the short man's cigar sharp in her nose.

Two nurses stood at the station on the fifth floor east, laughing and chatting with the nurse behind the desk. A man in a burgundy robe walked beside a tall woman in a business suit and tie.

Sheela walked to the end of the corridor and stopped, her legs suddenly weak and shaky. She tucked her tan blouse into the dark brown pants at her narrow waist. A warm jacket was draped over her arm. She wore a little eye makeup, a touch of blush, and pink lip gloss to try and hide how pale and tired she looked.

Could she walk up to Bobby's bed without fainting, without running away in terror?

She lifted her chin and squared her shoulders, then shifted her jacket to her other arm. With the tip of her tongue she moistened her dry lips. She pushed open the door and walked into the small room. A nurse looked up, then smiled and walked forward.

"You must be Sheela Jenkins. I'm Becky Tirrell. Wade said you'd be here one of these days."

Sheela forced a small smile as she kept her eyes glued to the red-haired, freckled nurse dressed in a white jumpsuit. "I won't be staying long." If she had the strength, she'd turn and run now.

Nurse Tirrell smiled in sympathy. "I know it's a shock to see your mother lying in a hospital bed with tubes in her. But it would help her if you could talk to her normally. I believe that she can hear even if she is in a coma. But please, speak positive, kind things."

Sheela walked to the narrow bed, her throat dry and her heart thudding painfully. Bobby looked old and pale. Even her red hair looked dull and lifeless. A scratch ran from the corner of her eye down to her chin. One leg was in a cast. Could this small, frail woman be the same one who had used anything within reach to beat her with?

"It's quite all right to speak to her," said Nurse Tirrell softly. "If you want, I can step outside the door for a minute."

Sheela shook her head. "No. No, stay." She would not, could not be in the room alone with Bobby.

The nurse walked to the corner and sat on the edge of a chair, her hands folded in her lap. The smell of the small room sickened Sheela. A bouquet of roses and baby's breath stood in a glass vase on the small table near the head of the bed.

Sheela stood at the side of the bed, her throat closed. Bobby's eyelids fluttered and Sheela gasped, then stumbled back. Nurse Tirrell was at her side immediately. She saw Bobby's eyelids flutter and she smiled.

"She's waking at last, I think. She must have felt you here."

With a strangled moan, Sheela turned and fled. In the hall she collided with a solid object and she looked up to find Aaron Brooks. She gasped and tried to pull back, but he gripped her arms. For the past few days they'd spoken about business only. She was shocked to see him in the hospital.

He saw her pale face and haunted eyes and his heart ached. "Is your mother worse?"

"What . . . what are you doing here?"

"I came to look in on your mother."

"Oh!"

He dropped his hands to his sides, then tugged on the knot of his tie. "I hope you don't mind."

She shook her head.

"I know it was hard on you to see her like that when you're used to seeing her laughing and talking."

How could he know what her memory of Bobby was? "I must . . . go."

"Let me buy you a cup of coffee."

She shook her head. "I'm . . . going home."

He flipped back his jacket and stood with his hands on his hips. "I want to help you."

"What can you do?"

"Keep you company."

She stiffened. "I don't need you. Or anybody!"

Her words stabbed sharply into his heart. "I'll be praying for you."

She swallowed hard, sorry for being so mean to him. "Thank you."

"And for your mother."

Sheela turned away just in time to see the elevator

door open. A short, plump women in her sixties, dressed in dark slacks and a dark wool coat walked out. The woman saw Sheela and momentarily hesitated.

Sheela gasped and stumbled but Aaron caught her arm before she fell.

"What?" he asked, his head close to hers.

"Grandmother," she whispered. "Oh, I can't bear to see her now."

"But why not?"

The woman rushed at Sheela. "Oh, Sheela!" She grabbed Sheela and hugged her before Sheela could escape. "I just now learned about Barbara. I wanted to see her and make sure she's all right."

Sheela pulled back. "She's just down the hall."

"Have you seen her?"

"Yes."

The woman glanced from Sheela to Aaron and back again.

"Grandmother, this is my boss Aaron Brooks. Aaron, Emma Hall, Bobby's mother." The words almost choked her. Why had she come? Her life was once again slipping out of her control.

Emma Hall held out her hand and Aaron clasped it warmly. "I'm glad to meet you, Mr. Brooks. You've been good to Sheela. I heard about you from my daughter." Emma shook her finger at Sheela. "This one won't come see me. I get a Christmas card from her and that's all."

"Don't, Grandmother."

Emma reached for Sheela's hand, but Sheela drew away and Emma shrugged. "I'm going to Barbara now. Want to come with me? I need you."

Sheela suddenly saw the deep lines in her grandmother's face and noticed how faded her brown eyes had become. She had turned into an old woman. "I'll walk as far as her room with you, but that's it. I'm on my way home."

Aaron considered leaving them alone, but he couldn't leave Sheela when she looked ready to drop. He fell into step beside them. "The doctor said that Mrs. Jenkins is holding her own."

Sheela shot a surprised look at Aaron. She hadn't realized he'd kept tabs on Bobby.

"I'm glad to hear that," said Emma. "I was so surprised about the accident. My Barbara is always full of life. I hate to think of her lying in a sick bed, so close to death." Emma shuddered.

Sheela's stomach churned in agitation. She'd often heard Bobby's stories of how Grandma had beat her, often enough to put her in the hospital. Now Grandma was sounding like they loved each other. She glanced over to find Aaron studying her closely. She flushed and he lifted a brow questioningly.

At Bobby's door Sheela said goodbye to her grandmother, but before she could walk away, the door opened.

"Bobby is awake!" exclaimed Nurse Tirrell with a wide smile. "And she knows who she is."

"We want to see her," said Emma. "I'm her mother."

Sheela backed away, then turned and fled.

Aaron watched her run and took a step to follow her, then sighed and shook his head. She wouldn't let him near her.

Emma touched his arm. "I see you have a soft spot for our Sheela. I'd like to talk to you if you can wait until I see Barbara."

He pushed his hand into his pocket and fingered his change. "I'll wait in the lounge a few doors down."

"I'll find you." Emma walked into the room and

Aaron watched the door close.

Did he have more than a soft spot for Sheela?

Abruptly he strode to the lounge and sank down on a comfortable platform rocker. The strong smell of cigarette ashes irritated his nose. The room was empty and he leaned his head back and closed his eyes. He hadn't been sleeping well lately with Sheela so much on his mind.

Her sad little face seemed glued to the inside of his eyelids. He prayed often for her and so had his family. They were concerned about Sheela. His mother had asked him to invite her to the family dinner Sunday.

A hand touched his arm and he jerked forward to find Emma Hall standing beside him, her face as gray as her hair.

"She looked real bad to me. The nurse wouldn't let me stay longer."

"Can I get you a cup of coffee?"

Emma sank to the couch next to the chair. "No. I need to talk to you. I can get coffee later when I drive home."

He leaned toward her, his hands locked between his knees. "I do want to help Sheela, Mrs. Hall."

"I know you do. I saw your face when you looked at her."

His heart jerked.

Emma rubbed her slacks at her knees. "Mr. Brooks, what I'm going to tell you is not pretty. It hurts me to talk about it, but I have to set things right in my life. I'm not young and thoughts of the past plague me."

Aaron frowned, wondering what could be so terrible in this ordinary-looking woman's life.

Emma held her purse against her plump body. Tears filled her dark eyes. "I don't know how to start."

"Are you sure you want to tell me?"

"Yes. Because you care about our Sheela."

"Then just start wherever you can."

Emma bit her lower lip and sighed raggedly. "When Barbara . . . was still with me . . . I beat . . . her. My little Barbara." Her voice died and she sniffed.

Aaron gripped the arms of the chair and waited for her to continue.

She cleared her throat and picked at the sleeve of her coat. "I had a rough life and I couldn't handle it. I took it out on my poor girl. I didn't know it was because I needed emotional help until she was grown and gone from me. One day I saw it on the TV about child abuse." She dabbed her eyes with a tissue from her purse. "Oh, I can't go on!"

"Yes, you can."

Emma drew a ragged breath. "Barbara got married when she was seventeen. She was pregnant and she was afraid to tell me. They ran off and got married. The boy was only eighteen. I know she married him just to get away from me."

Aaron gripped the arms of the rocker.

Emma looked unseeingly across the small room. "They had Sheela. She was less than a year old when . . . when Barbara first . . . beat her."

Shock rocked Aaron. "Beat her?" he asked hoarsely.

"I warned her that she might kill her, and she said she'd stop. Then Herb just walked out when Sheela was five. Barbara lived with me for a while but my nerves couldn't take it and she moved out on her own."

Aaron sat very still, his stomach a tight, hard knot.

"Barbara beat Sheela more and more. They had to move a lot so Barbara wouldn't lose her." Emma looked earnestly at Aaron. "She loves Sheela. Just like I love her." Emma blew her nose and seemed to shrink into herself. "Our Sheela pulled into a shell and she won't let no one in. She won't go out with men for fear of falling in love. She said she'll never have babies in case she might beat them. She said she won't have anything to do with me or Barbara as long as she lives. She won't let anyone close so she don't get hurt." Tears streamed down Emma's ashen cheeks. "She can't keep on living like that."

"I feel so badly for her. For all of you!"

Emma nodded. "Me too. I'm telling you all this so you can help our Sheela. I know you like her and I know you've been working together for three years. If anyone can help her, you can. It's too late for me and maybe for Barbara too. But not for Sheela."

Aaron reached out and took Emma's plump, rough hand in his. "Mrs. Hall, I promise that I'll do what I can for Sheela. But right now I want to help you."

"You . . . can't. No one can."

He patted her hand. "God can and will help you, Mrs. Hall. He loves you and wants to help you."

She shook her head and sniffed. "He can't forgive me for what I did to my girl. You just go help Sheela and that'll be answer enough for me."

"No. No, it's not enough for you. God wants to help you too. He is ready to forgive and forget when you ask Him to. He sent Jesus to you." Aaron talked quietly and as he talked he saw hope fill Emma's eyes.

"I heard a man on TV talk about Jesus and I almost turned my life over to Him, but I knew I'd been too bad."

"No one's too bad that God can't forgive him. You are precious to Him."

"How can that be true?"

"The Bible says that God loved you so much that

He sent Jesus to take your sins from you so that you could live—live an abundant life."

"It seems too good to be true."

Aaron patted her arm. "Mrs. Hall, in the Bible in 1 John 1:9 it says, 'If we confess our sins, our wrong doings, he is faithful and just to forgive us our sins, and to cleanse us from all unrighteousness.' He'll forgive and make you clean as if you never did . . . did beat your daughter."

Fresh tears streamed down Emma's cheeks. "Can it be true?"

"Yes. Matthew 10:32 says that whoever confesses Jesus before men, Jesus will confess before his Father God in heaven." Aaron sat on the edge of his chair. "Mrs. Hall, Jesus wants you to give yourself to Him so He can take away your old nature and put a new heart, a clean heart in you."

"Oh, I want to!"

"Shall we pray now?"

"Yes!"

Aaron prayed with her and saw her born into the kingdom of God. She lifted a shining face and tears ran down her wrinkled cheeks.

"I will never forget this day, Mr. Brooks. I'm forgiven!"

"Yes, you are."

"Now, we'll help Barbara and Sheela."

"Yes, we will."

Emma wiped her tears. "I asked for help for Sheela and found help myself. What a miracle!"

"Do you have a Bible?"

"Yes."

"I want you to read it every day for strength and help. The Bible is God's Word for us to show us how to live. It's food for your spirit. Start in the Book of John and then go from there."

"I'll tell Barbara that I am forgiven at long last, and I'll ask her to forgive me. This time I'll mean it." Emma slipped on her coat with Aaron's help. Her eyes sparkled as she looked up at him. "Oh, I am so happy!"

"So am I! God does work miracles!"

"For Sheela and Barbara, too."

"Yes." Aaron hugged Emma, then walked her to her car. A cool wind whistled through the trees near the parking lot. Cars drove past on the street that led downtown.

Aaron slowly walked to his car and slipped inside. The smell of leather was pleasant. "I must tell Sheela!" He wanted to tell her now tonight about her grandmother, but he knew she wouldn't talk to him. Tomorrow at work he'd take her to his office and tell her what he knew about her past and her future. With God's help he'd crack her shell so that she could never again hide from him.

"Sheela, you don't know it yet, but your life is starting to change." He leaned back in his seat and laughed, then suddenly sobered as he thought of the little girl who had suffered so much while she was growing up.

Tears pricked his eyes as he gripped the steering wheel. "Heavenly Father, in Jesus' Name, right now, tonight, surround Sheela with your peace and give her a good night's rest. Prepare her heart to hear about you and your love. Help me to share you with her. And help her to receive. Send other believers across her path to help her find you."

Several minutes later he let himself into his apartment. "Tomorrow, Sheela. We'll talk tomorrow."

Chapter 8

he was twelve years old.

She leaned back on the couch and crossed her arms, trying to get interested in Sunday morning cartoons on a sunny May morning. The smell of the toast she'd burned still hung in the air. She curled her legs under her and rubbed her hand down her jeans, then tugged her flannel shirt in place. Impatiently she pushed her long brown hair out of her face. She should've brushed it and pinned it back.

The phone rang and she jumped nervously, then shot a look toward Bobby's closed bedroom door. Her hand trembled as she reached for the phone. By stretching, she didn't have to move off the couch.

"Hello." Her voice quivered and she scowled.

"This is Carl Lacey. Is Bobby up yet?"

"No. Should I wake her?"

"No. Just tell her that I called. Carl Lacey. Can you remember that?"

"Yes." Who was Carl Lacey?

"Tell her that I called and to call me back before ten-thirty. We made plans last night, but I need her to call before ten-thirty or it'll be too late."

"I'll tell her." Sheela hung up and settled back to watch TV. A woman who reminded her of her sixth grade teacher was telling a Bible story. Children sat around her feet and looked as if they were enjoying the story. Sheela leaned forward to catch every word.

"In the Bible it says that Jesus loved to have the children come to Him. He helped them with their problems. He healed their sicknesses. He taught them to love. He loved them. Once Jesus raised a little girl from the dead."

"Jesus is alive in heaven right now and he still does what He did in the Bible. He still loves each one of you and He still wants to help you. He is your friend."

Sheela listened with her whole heart as the woman told of Jesus' death on the cross and His burial, then of being raised from the dead to live forevermore.

A warmth spread inside Sheela and she smiled. Could it really be possible that Jesus cared for her and that He'd protect her and keep her safe?

Just then the bedroom door opened and Bobby walked out, yawning and tying the belt to her shabby pink robe. Her red hair was tousled and her cheeks pink. She stared at the TV. "What on earth are you watching, Sheela? I can't believe that you'd sit there and listen to that stuff about Jesus. I was told all that and I thought it was true, but He sure never helped me when I needed help." Impatiently she clicked off the set and dropped to the couch beside Sheela. "You and me aren't Sunday School types, Shee. We want more out of life. We want excitement and money and love! We don't want that made-up stuff that doesn't work. We got each other and that's all we need."

Sheela thought of the families she'd seen and she wanted to say that she wanted to be in a happy family and go to church and learn about Jesus, but she sat quietly.

A car backfired and she jumped. Bobby frowned and shook her head.

"You shouldn't be so nervous at your age. Learn to relax like me." She pushed herself up. "I want a cup of coffee. I just can't wake up until I've had my first cup of coffee." Bobby chatted on and on about how they'd live when she finally found the right rich man. "I could even send you to a private school so you'll have the best of everything. Would you like that?"

Sheela nodded because Bobby expected it of her, but she couldn't imagine going away from Momma to a private school. Hope rose in her, then she flushed with guilt. She shouldn't want to leave her own mother.

She looked at the clock beside the stove and her heart dropped to her feet. It was eleven o'clock. She locked her icy fingers together. "I forgot to tell you that you had a phone call while you were asleep." Her mouth felt almost too dry to talk.

"I thought I heard the phone. Who was it?" Bobby walked toward the phone, another cup of steaming coffee in her hand.' "Carl Lacey said to call him back."

Bobby grinned and rolled her eyes. "Oh, Carl! What a man!"

Fear pricked Sheela's skin and she pushed back tight into the corner of the couch. If she suddenly left, Bobby would suspect something and force her back.

Bobby perched on the arm of the couch and hummed softly as she dialed. Slowly the pleased look was replaced with a frown. "Why isn't he answering?" She let it ring a few more times, tapping her toe impatiently. "Hi, Carl. What took you so long to answer? I'll be ready whenever you say."

Sheela clutched the afghan next to her. She couldn't look at Bobby as she talked to Carl. Finally Bobby slammed down the receiver and whirled on Sheela.

"You should be scared, Sheela Jenkins! You know how bad you are, don't you? Carl made other plans. Other plans! He said he was sorry, but when he didn't hear from me by ten-thirty, he knew I didn't want to go sailing, so he made other plans. Can you imagine?" Bobby tugged at her hair with both hands. "Oh! Oh, I could scream! How can I spend a whole boring Sunday by myself?"

Sheela shivered and tried to sink out of sight. Bobby grabbed her by the wrist and jerked her up.

"You'll be very sorry, little girl. After this you'll remember to give me my phone messages on time. You'll remember all right."

Sheela tugged, but Bobby's grip tightened. "Don't, Momma!"

Bobby slapped Sheela across the cheek. A pink mark appeared and then a welt. "I told you to call me Bobby, didn't I?"

"Bobby," whispered Sheela.

"I'm so angry at you, Sheela! I wanted to go with Carl Lacey, but now I can't because of you. You! What can I do to make you remember important messages? What can I do so that you'll remember this day forever?" Bobby flung Sheela from her, then stood over her where she lay on the dusty floor.

Sheela cringed, but didn't dare move even a finger.

"Momma made me remember to run right to her to tell her if someone was coming for a surprise visit." Bobby rubbed the scar at the side of her face near her ear. "She made me sit on the porch or at the front window and watch to see if anyone was coming until she had everything in the house just the way she wanted it. But one day I went off to play with a girl down the street from us. Mikki Lowe. We played dolls. She had so many dolls and I had only one." A faraway look came in Bobby's eyes and Sheela glanced toward the bathroom door and safety. But Bobby shook herself and continued. "And one of the neighbor ladies came and she saw Momma's house in a mess and Momma was angry at me. She said that I was very bad. She said that she would make me remember to keep watch for her." Bobby whimpered and Sheela shivered, her eyes wide in terror. "I won't ever forget no matter what. I got this to remember." She rubbed the scar again. "I bet this is why no man wants to marry me."

"Don't, Bobby," whispered Sheela. "Don't get mad and cut me."

Bobby laughed hysterically. "Do you think I'm that cruel? I wouldn't do that to you. But I'll find a way to punish you." She looked around, found an extension cord and Sheela closed her eyes and moaned. She felt the blow even before Bobby struck.

The next morning Sheela opened her eyes and looked up at the ceiling of her tiny bedroom. A water spot shaped like a dog with floppy ears was directly over her head. The landlord had said that he'd fix the leak in the roof, but he never had.

She tried to move. Pain shot through her body and a scream caught in her throat.

Bobby poked her head in the door and Sheela froze. "Why aren't you up yet? You have to go to school."

Sheela clutched the sheet. "I can't get up. I . . . hurt too much."

"Hurt? I didn't do anything to make you hurt that much." Bobby buttoned her yellow jacket, then touched the scar beside her ear. "I'm nothing like Momma. You're lucky that I'm your momma, and not Grandma. She did terrible things to me. Terrible things. I only give you what you deserve. Now, get up! I'll give you to the count of five."

"I . . . can't move."

"Oh, all right! Stay in bed!" Bobby turned and walked away. Sheela's face crumpled and she sobbed quietly into her blanket.

Suddenly, with a jerk Sheela sat forward. She blinked and looked around. She was not twelve years old. She was twenty-four, living on her own away from Bobby. The pain she felt was not new bruises, but deep scars that could never be healed. She leaped up, her heart thudding painfully against her chest.

She paced her apartment, her stomach churning with agony. Would she ever be able to forget her past? Seeing Bobby and Grandma tonight had made things much worse for her. She tugged at her hair and moaned in despair. She must never see Bobby again. She must once again push the past deep inside and lock it away.

What if Aaron learned the truth about her? Would he send her packing or would he pity her? Oh, she didn't want him to do either!

She ran water into the teakettle, then set it on a front burner to boil. Maybe a cup of tea would settle her nerves a little.

Slowly she unbottoned her tan blouse and slipped on her blue robe that almost brushed the thin carpet. The clock beside her bed ticked loudly. Muted traffic sounds reached through the front window. The tea-kettle whistled and she jumped.

A few minutes later she sat at the small table and sipped the tea. Why had she suddenly remembered seeing that TV program with the woman sharing Jesus? A deep yearning to hear about Him again rose inside her. Did He really love her and care for her?

No. No, it was wishful thinking.

She cupped her hands around her white mug and stared unseeingly across the small room. The only colorful thing in the room was the single red rosebud made of silk that Addie had given her two days ago. It didn't fit in with her dull life, her empty, loveless life.

She frowned. Her life wasn't exactly dull, nor without love. Addie cared for her and she'd grown very fond of Addie. Thoughts of Aaron flashed in her mind. She worked for Brooks Advertising. Aaron was a fine man as long as he didn't get too close, but he had been pushing into her life too much lately.

Impatiently she shoved back the chair and stood, almost spilling her tea. What happened that her life was suddenly in turmoil again? She'd worked so hard to keep it a blank canvas.

With long steps she paced the room, wringing her hands. Somehow she had to get back a facade of calmness. She must push thoughts of Bobby and Grandma and even Aaron to the far corner of her mind.

She glanced at the clock and frowned. She must get to bed and to sleep. Tomorrow was Friday with a heavy work load. Don might miss work again because of Roxie.

With jerky movements Sheela slipped on her paja-mas, brushed her teeth and cleaned her face. Her eyes looked too large for her face. Dark smudges under each eye made them look more gray than blue. Her cheeks were pale and her hair a wild mess. She had to bring back the ice maiden that she'd become since she left business college to go to work. But how could she do it?

Could she push Aaron to the back of her mind? Did she honestly want to?

She crept into bed without finding an answer. She closed her eyes and suddenly a calmness descended on her like she had never experienced before. It was as if someone had suddenly taken away her worries and left a peace in their place. She turned on her side and slept.

The next morning she sailed into her office, feeling more rested than she had in a long, long time. She slipped off her coat and hung it in the closet. Don walked in, whistling.

Sheela turned with a smile. "Roxie must be better."

Don nodded. "The doctor said the baby could come any day."

"But I thought he said December."

"He did, but he said he was off a little. He said that Roxie is suffering from tension and that she should get her mind off the birth date and plan the nursery. Roxie's busy fixing it up. She was going to wait until she saw if it was a boy or girl, but now she's fixing it for either."

"Good. I'm sure you're feeling better too."

"You're right. Now, I can get to work properly." He walked to his office and closed his door.

In his office Aaron heard Sheela and he strode across the room and flung wide his door. "Good morning!"

She turned and smiled and a glad light leaped in her eyes.

He saw the light, and his heart raced, but he didn't

say anything that might frighten her. She looked pretty in her gray plaid jacket, plain gray skirt and a white blouse with a strand of red beads. He wanted to catch her close to his heart and tell her she was safe. "You look rested," he said softly.

"I am. For the first time in a long time I slept soundly."

"Praise God."

When she'd first started working for him, a statement like that had alarmed her, but now she expected it.

"I prayed for you last night."

"You did?"

"Yes, that you'd have a restful, peaceful night."

She smiled. "Your prayers were answered." She must remember to tell Jill.

He walked toward her and stopped just a foot from her. He caught a whiff of her perfume and he liked it. "I called the hospital today and found another prayer was answered. Your mother is doing much better. The doctor said she's going to recover."

The smile vanished and Sheela walked stiffly to her desk and sank down on her chair. She didn't want to hear about Bobby. "I'd better get to work."

"The boss will allow you a couple more minutes of free time."

"That's not necessary."

Aaron perched on the corner of her desk. "I have good news about your grandmother, too."

"I don't want to hear it."

"You'll be happy about this."

She frowned at him. "Can't you understand yet that I don't want to hear about my mother or my grandmother?"

Aaron pushed himself up and smiled. "Your grandmother accepted Jesus into her life. She's a new woman in Christ. Her sins are gone, forgiven and forgotten."

"Not by me! Not ever by me!" Sheela clamped her lips closed tightly. She shouldn't have said that, but it was out and she couldn't make Aaron forget the words.

He'd planned on taking her to his office to talk to her about God in her life, but he knew she wasn't ready to listen. He walked to his door and turned to face her. She waited for a sharp answer from him or even anger. The warm look in his eyes pierced through the ice around her heart.

"I'm glad you work for me, Sheela. You're a wonderful woman and a very special person." He smiled and walked into his office.

She leaned back in her chair and covered her racing heart with an unsteady hand. He had been serious. He thought she was a wonderful woman! A special person!

The phone rang and she scooped it up and answered with a lilt in her voice.

"Sheela, it's Lillian Ketchum, dear. I know I shouldn't bother you at work, but I had to call someone."

She closed her eyes. "What's wrong, Mrs. Ketchum?"

"It's Addie. She walked home from school a few minutes ago and she says she won't go back. Her mom's not home and I have a touch of the flu. What should I do?"

"Is Addie sick?"

"No. She won't tell me what's wrong."

Sheela ran a finger over her stapler. "Can By Windfield watch her?"

"He would if he were here, but he took . . . took . . . Nadia out for a walk. And just in time, too. Zelda searched the place again for a cat." Mrs. Ketchum's last words were whispered and Sheela could barely hear.

Sheela thought for a while. "Send Addie here to me." Surely Aaron wouldn't mind. "She can stay with me until Jill gets home. Addie knows the way. We walked by here a few days ago when we were out for a walk together."

"Oh, thank you, dear! I'll send her right over. If she's not in your office in just a short time, you let me know. I'd hate for anything to happen to her. I feel so responsible for her."

"She's lucky to have a friend like you."

"And like you."

Sheela smiled. She hadn't planned on letting anyone into her heart, but somehow Addie had crept in unawares. "Don't you worry about Addie. Go upstairs and rest. Leave a note on Jill's door, telling her Addie's with me and to pick her up."

"I will. And thank you, Sheela. I'll talk to you when you get home."

"Bye." Sheela hung up and glanced toward Aaron's closed door. Should she tell him that Addie was coming? She shook her head. Why bother him? She rolled a piece of paper into her typewriter. If she could finish the correspondence and filing she could take Addie out for a walk and try to find out why she'd left school.

Several minutes later Addie walked in, her face red from running. She stopped beside Sheela's desk, smelling like fresh, cold air. "Are you mad at me for coming?"

"Of course not! Let me take your jacket."

Addie handed it over. She tugged her green sweatshirt down over her jeans. Her clothes were dirty and her hair uncombed. "I hate school!"

"You do?" Sheela hung the jacket and turned back to Addie. "Why?"

"I just do."

"Why don't you sit down here?" Sheela set the straight back chair beside her desk. "And you can draw while I work." She slid paper, pencil and markers over to the empty spot that she'd cleared off for Addie.

Addie sat down and crossed her arms. "I'll just sit here."

"All right. I just didn't want you to be bored." Sheela finished filing and turned to her typing. Occasionally she peeked under her long lashes at Addie. Finally Addie picked up a marker and drew a tiny red flower on the white paper. Soon she was bent over the desk, covering the page with artwork.

Aaron stepped out of his office, his black leather briefcase in his hand. "Sheela." He stopped short. "What have we here?"

Addie jumped up and ran to press against Sheela's side.

Butterflies fluttered in Sheela's stomach. "Aaron, this is Addie Konikof. I told you that I baby-sit her at times. She came home from school early and Mrs. Ketchum couldn't watch her. I said it was all right for her to come here. Addie, this is my boss, Aaron Brooks." Sheela waited uneasily for Aaron's answer.

He smiled and held out his hand to Addie. "I'm glad to meet you, Addie."

She shyly shook his hand, but didn't speak.

"You're a good artist, Addie. Maybe someday you'll come work for me. I can always use talent and willing workers."

Addie smiled and leaned harder against Sheela.

"I don't know how long Addie will be here, Aaron."

"It doesn't matter at all, Sheela. Don and I have a meeting at Greyson's and won't be back until after lunch. Will you be all right here alone with Addie?"

"Yes."

"Take Addie to lunch later if you want. On me." He dropped a twenty dollar bill in front of her. "Just click on the answering machine and lock the door when you leave."

Sheela nodded. Aaron never ceased to surprise her. She'd expected him to suggest that Addie go home as soon as possible. She didn't want to take his money, but she wanted less to argue over it. She slipped it in her drawer to put in her purse later.

"It was nice meeting you, Addie. I'll see you later." He winked at her and she smiled shyly. He turned to Sheela and smiled into her eyes. "Take care."

She nodded. She watched him walk to Don's door and open it.

"Ready, Don?"

"Ready." He walked out, his jacket in one hand, briefcase in the other. "Sheela, if Roxie calls and needs me, tell her I'm at Greyson's."

"I will."

"I'll call her at lunch time to let her know where I'm eating."

"All right."

"Don and his wife are expecting their first baby," Aaron told Addie. "He's a little nervous."

Don laughed and slapped Aaron on the back. "Just wait until it's you, my friend."

"I might skip the first and go right for the second just to keep from being so nervous." Aaron laughed and walked out with Don.

"He's nice," said Addie.

"He is," said Sheela, still looking at the closed door.

"Is he married?"

"No."

Addie slipped her arms around Sheela's neck. "You should marry him."

Sheela flushed. "I think I'd better get back to work."

"I still think you should marry him."

"Oh, Addie."

Addie kissed Sheela's cheek. "I love you, Sheela."

"Thank you. I . . . I love you, too." How long had it been since she'd said those words? Probably fourth grade when she'd told Mike that she loved him. Sheela held Addie close for a long time.

"I wish you were my mom."

"Oh, Addie, no!"

"Mom is mean to me sometimes."

Sheela couldn't bear to hear what Addie wanted to say. "Tell me why you left school today."

Addie sat on her chair and poked out her bottom lip.

"Well?"

"I hate school! They made fun of me."

"Who did?"

"Peggy and Lisa."

"Why?"

"Because I wear dirty clothes to school and because . . . my mom acts so funny when she visits school." Addie's face turned bright red.

"Funny? In what way?"

"Oh, she tries to act like she's a little girl. But she's not! She's old!"

Sheela remembered feeling the same about Bobby. Bobby had always tried to be one of the girls when she'd visited school. It had been very embarrassing. Sheela took Addie's hand in hers. "Your mom is only trying to make you proud of her." Sheela stopped. Had Bobby acted that way for the same reason? It felt strange to understand Bobby even in a small way.

"She doesn't care what I think of her!"

"But she does! She loves you!"

"No! She doesn't!"

"She told me she does, and I believe her."

"Then why does she..." Addie stopped and turned away.

"What?"

"Nothing." Addie's voice was almost too low for Sheela to hear.

"Tell me."

"I can't."

Sheela shuddered. Finally she said, "Let's get to work so we can go for lunch later."

Addie lifted haunted eyes to Sheela. "Do you really want me to tell you?"

Sheela bit her bottom lip. "No. No, I guess I don't."

"I didn't think so." Addie's eyes filled with tears and she blinked hard.

Sheela ducked her head and tried to concentrate on the letter she was typing.

Chapter 9

heela stood in front of her TV with the yellow plastic laundry basket resting lightly on her hip as she watched Aaron's ad for the Sundowner Restaurant. She smiled and nodded, pleased with what she saw. The ad was soon over and she clicked off the set and rubbed a hand across the top of it. She bought it last year just to watch Aaron's commercials in color. It was as if he made a brief visit in her dreary life even when she was alone. She'd be very embarrassed if he ever learned how avidly she watched his ads or how much she enjoyed watching him think them up. She would see the slight pucker between his fine brows and the narrowing of his green eyes and know that his brain was whirling with thoughts. At times he'd sit back with his feet propped on the corner of his desk, his ankles crossed and his eyes closed. At an inspiration, he'd drop his feet, shoot from the chair and share his

thoughts with her. She took them down and later typed them up for him to flesh out.

With a sigh she walked from her room and down to the basement laundry room. The sour smell made her wrinkle her nose. It was Zelda's job to see that the laundry room was kept clean, but she was too busy keeping her appearance perfect to bother. When she wasn't doing her nails or her hair, she was exercising or putting a mud pack on her unlined face. Lately she'd used her valuable time to hunt down the cat she was sure was in the building. So far she hadn't found it. Sheela smiled. "And she won't."

Sheela stuffed her clothes into two washers, poured in the detergent and slipped the coins in place. Water rushed into the tubs as she walked to a chair against the cold block wall. She frowned at the white fluffy robe lying in a heap on a chair beside her. It wasn't safe to forget anything in the laundry room. Once she left a new pair of jeans for no more than fifteen minutes. Sheela never found them again and when she reported them missing to Zelda, she'd said that she wasn't responsible for lost or stolen items.

Sheela opened her book but didn't see the words. She missed Addie more than she thought possible. Yesterday Jill had picked her up from the office with a breezy, "Hope she wasn't any bother. We're going away for the weekend with friends. Be back Sunday night late."

Addie had hugged her and kissed her before Jill rushed her away.

"Goodbye, Addie," Sheela had whispered at the closed door. It had been a long time before she could concentrate on her work.

Aaron had called and said he couldn't make it back to the office and asked her to lock up for him.

She sighed. She wouldn't see him until Monday.

The door opened and she looked up to see Byron Windfield walking in with his laundry. He stopped at the sight of her and his face reddened, then he grinned sheepishly. She knew he had Nadia.

"Hello, Sheela." He had the small, wiry body of a gymnast and even at seventy years old he was in better physical condition than most people. He had sparse gray hair and a well-trimmed gray beard. "You won't tell on me for bringing Nadia with me, will you?"

Sheela sighed, but shook her head. "Mr. Windfield, you know what Zelda will do if she catches you with Nadia."

"Call me By. Everybody does." He piled his clothes in one washer while his soft white cat wound in and out of his legs, her fluffy white tail high and her back arched. Sheela could hear her purring over the sloshing of the water in the washers.

"You must be careful of Zelda, By."

"Me and Nadia won't be here much longer, Sheela. I heard that my place will be available next month."

Sheela closed her book. "You said that last month."

"But they said the people who are there now will be out for sure." He pushed his coins in, then turned and leaned against the washer, his ankles crossed. "I put in for that place five months ago when I heard that it was available. I put my money down. I can keep Nadia there without getting into trouble." He grinned mischievously. "Not that Nadia and me would ever get into trouble. What would an old gymnast and his cat do to make trouble for anyone?"

"Tell that to Zelda." Sheela chuckled.

"Zelda won't find Nadia. Even if she did she

couldn't do anything. She knows I'm leaving as soon as the condo's free."

"I don't think that'll stop Zelda. She's out to see fur fly." Sheela copied Zelda's tone and voice and they both laughed.

"I saw a young man drive you home the other day. Is that your young man?"

Sheela gripped her book tighter. "He's my boss."

"Oh." By narrowed his eyes. "Too bad he's not your fellow."

Sheela moved restlessly.

"I didn't mean to pry."

"That's all right."

Nadia meowed and By scooped her up, crooning softly to her. Soon she was purring happily with her great head against his shoulder.

Sheela had wanted a cat when she was young, but Bobby had not allowed her to have any pet. She sighed heavily.

By wagged a thin finger at Sheela. "It's not right for a young girl to keep to herself as much as you do, Sheela. You need to get out and meet people your age. Make friends. I've never seen you talk to anyone in this building but me, Lillian, Addie and Jill. And you wouldn't do that if me and Lillian hadn't forced ourselves on you. But then I'm forgetting our own Zelda." He grinned. "You need more than us."

She crossed her legs and leaned on her knee. "I want my life the way it is, By."

"Sure you do." His voice was heavy with sarcasm. "And I like to hide Nadia every time anyone comes along. I like to be deceitful. Sure I do."

"Don't, By," she whispered raggedly.

"I'm sorry, little girl."

A noise outside the door startled them both. Nadia

leaped to the floor and By stood frozen with his eyes glued to the door. Quick as a flash Sheela grabbed the fluffy white robe and scooped up Nadia and dropped them in her basket.

Zelda walked in and stopped just inside the door. "I've been looking for you, Byron Windfield!" It was an accusation. Her red curls were in perfect order and her tall, sleek dancer's body was covered with a black leotard and black wrap-around skirt. The red of her long nails and full lips matched her hair color.

"I've been here with Sheela," said By as if he didn't have a care in the world. "Did you want something special?"

Zelda's hazel eyes narrowed into thin slits of suspicion. "Grace Keeler in 101 says she saw you with a big white cat."

Sheela darted a look at the basket. The white robe moved and was still.

By laughed and shook his head. "Isn't Grace Keeler the woman with the pop bottle bottoms for glasses?"

Zelda snorted. "I'll admit that her eyesight isn't very good, but I had to check out her story. It's part of my job."

"So is cleaning this room," said By. "Why don't you do it now?"

Sheela sat very still.

"I don't have time now!" Zelda squared her shoulders. "I'm looking for a cat."

"If I had a cat, wouldn't Sheela have noticed? She'd never let me have a cat when she knows how you feel."

Zelda turned her sharp eyes on Sheela, shrugged and looked away. "By Windfield, don't ever get it in your head that you can have an animal in my place. I follow the rules or I'm out of a job. And I need this job while I'm waiting to get back to New York." She swirled her skirt as she turned out the door. "Nothing funny goes on in my building." She pushed the door shut with a bang.

Sheela looked at By and saw his lips twitch with laughter. She grinned at him. Nadia meowed and pushed her nose out of the folds of the robe.

"You can come out now, my girl. Zelda won't be back again today. Or tomorrow. She wouldn't come down here more than once a week." He laughed. "I was surprised to see her today."

"I wish she'd noticed the bad smell and done something about it. We should get Grace Keeler to report it."

They laughed together and Sheela's loneliness suddenly vanished.

By patted her arm. "Thanks from Nadia and me both. I couldn't get along without Nadia, not even for a few days. I didn't want to move in here, but it was all I could find until my place is ready."

"You'll have to be more careful with Nadia."

"I know. But it won't be long now. I've been trying to get Lillian to get out of here with me, but she can't afford to, she said."

Sheela pushed her clothes into the dryer. "I wish she would go with you."

"You should leave too. This is no place for you, Sheela. Why don't you get out of here?"

"It's all right for my needs."

"I've lived in a lot of places, some of them worse than this, but most better. You would enjoy life more if your surroundings were attractive and pleasant smelling." He sat on a chair and Nadia leaped on his lap. "You need to do something to put a sparkle in your eye."

Something hard struck against the dryer as it

whirled around. She turned away from By, opening the dryer and hunting around until she found the hard object. It was a nickel, almost too hot to touch. She pushed it into her jeans and closed the door again.

"You need a husband and children."

She turned back, her eyes full of pain. "Don't, By. Tell me about your condo. Please."

"If that's the way you want it, Sheela." He stroked his gray beard. "I don't have to fall off the parallel bars before I know when to quit. You're a fine girl, Sheela, but I know you have a deep pain that's eating away inside you and I just wish that I could do something to help you."

She turned from him, fighting against betraying tears.

"You know, I think I'd better take Nadia to my room before somebody sees her. Will you watch my stuff?"

"Yes."

He hesitated at the door. "You're a fine girl, Sheela. You deserve to be happy."

When the door closed after him she sniffed back tears. Aaron had said she was special and By had said she was fine. Neither was true.

The washer stopped and she stuck By's clothes in the dryer and pushed in the coins from her pocket. She knew he'd insist on paying her back. He didn't want to be obligated to anyone.

Sheela folded her clothes that were almost too hot to touch. A nylon slip clung to her pillowcase and she pulled them apart, listening to the crackle and watching the sparks fly. When she went shopping she'd buy something to take out the static cling. Glancing at her watch, she remembered that Lillian Ketchum planned to walk to the grocery store with her this afternoon. She'd buy a few cans of cat food for Nadia. By couldn't object to a gift for his beloved cat. Sheela knew his money was tied up in his condo and that often he was short of food. He always made sure Nadia had plenty to eat even when he didn't.

By walked in, whistling a merry tune. He stopped when he saw his clothes in the dryer. "I got the right change. You take it." He handed it to her and she reluctantly pocketed it. "I got Nadia back to my room safe and sound. She curled up on my pillow and fell asleep. I might do the same when I finish here."

"Mrs. Ketchum and I are going shopping later. Do you want me to pick up anything for you?"

"No. My check should come Monday or Tuesday and then I'll go shopping."

"I can lend you money until then if you need it."

He drew himself up and he was still shorter than Sheela. "I can take care of myself."

"I know." A warm feeling for him curled around her heart and surprised her. Was she beginning to care for him just as she did Addie? The thought surprised her. She picked up her basket. "I'll see you later. Why don't you bring Nadia and have tea with Mrs. Ketchum and me later?"

"I might do that. I have a few crackers I could bring."

"Save them. I have some that need to be eaten before they get stale." She knew that was the only way she could get him to keep his crackers for himself.

"See you later then."

She smiled and walked out of the room with her clean, folded laundry in the yellow plastic basket resting against her hip. The job was done for another Saturday.

Later in the grocery store she stopped at the cat food.

Lillian Ketchum tapped her arm. "I'm buying cat food, dear. You save your money for yourself."

Sheela knew Mrs. Ketchum didn't have money to spare. "I want to buy Nadia a gift. May I, please, Mrs. Ketchum?"

"Please, dear, try to remember to call me Lillian. We are friends."

Sheela smiled and set six cans of cat food in her cart. "I do want to buy the cat food." Lillian didn't object further and Sheela pushed her cart forward. She stopped next at the cereal. "I always have trouble deciding what cereal to buy."

"My, dear, I don't think you should get any of this. It has too much sugar in it. Just down the aisle is some with natural grains and nuts and raisins. That's much better for you. Much better. You're slender, dear, but you want to be healthy too. Sugar is harmful to you. Harmful."

"I know. I just never tried granola." She lifted down the box and studied the ingredients, then put two boxes in her cart. Later she'd give one to Lillian, when she could say she couldn't eat it before it spoiled.

"What about vegetables, dear? I think fresh broccoli would be good. Do you know how to make cheese sauce? If not, I'll teach you."

"I'd better stick to frozen."

Lillian pushed ahead and stopped at the carrots. Her long coat flapped open. Thin legs and feet encased in winter boots, stuck out below the tweed wool coat that had seen better days. Her hands were thin and covered with age spots. Deep wrinkles lined her round face and her white hair was cut short and waved. Her snapping blue eyes didn't seem to miss anything. She stuck a bag of carrots in her cart. She held up another bag. "Sheela?"

She nodded. They walked together down each aisle. Sheela stopped beside the cookies. "I'd like to get some to go with our tea this afternoon."

"That would be good, dear. Just not too many."

"No. Not too many. How about a bag of Oreos?"

Lillian smiled. "You know I can't resist Oreos, don't you?"

"Yes." Sheela saw the pleased look on Lillian's face and it warmed her heart. Lillian would make a wonderful grandmother. Sheela gripped her cart tighter.

She bit her lower lip. She would not think about Grandmother or Bobby.

Later at home she quickly put away her groceries and carried the cookies and cat food to Lillian's. By and Lillian sat at the table with cups of tea with Nadia at By's feet.

"Show By what you bought for Nadia," said Lillian, glowing with pride.

"What did you get her?" asked By with a scowl.

"A gift. It is her birthday, isn't it?" Sheela grinned and finally By did too.

"Let's see what you got her."

Sheela handed him the bag and he opened it and peeked inside. Tears filled his eyes and he swallowed hard.

"Come here, Nadia. See what Sheela Jenkins gave you. You're going to eat as well as Morris. But you're much prettier than that TV cat, and you aren't as finicky."

Nadia purred and rubbed against the bag.

"She likes it and says thank you." By cleared his throat. "You're a good girl, Sheela."

Sheela drew back.

"You're embarrassing the girl, By." Lillian poured his cup full of tea again and filled Sheela's cup. "Just put the cat food away and tell us about your condo."

By scowled at her. "Why is it you think you can get me off the subject by bringing up my condo?"

"It's worked before," said Lillian.

"Yah?"

"Yes."

"Well, not this time."

Sheela looked at the two across from each other and enjoyed listening to them talk back and forth. Right now she felt years older than either of them. Finally she allowed them to draw her into their conversation. Before long Lillian mentioned Jill.

"I think she needs help," said By.

"What kind of help?" asked Sheela guardedly.

"Professional help. I think she is too hard on Addie."

Lillian sniffed. "Too hard? She leaves bruises."

Sheela shook her head. "I don't think we should be talking about them. It's not our business."

"Whose business is it then?" asked By.

"I've tried to talk to Jill," said Lillian. But she puts up her guard and I can't get past it. Addie won't confide in me. Does she in you, Sheela?"

"She talks to me, but she hasn't said anything bad about her mother's treatment of her." Sheela pushed aside the thoughts of what Addie had tried to tell her.

"Something has to be done and soon," said Lillian.

"Yes, it does," said By. He looked right at Sheela.

"Not me! I'm not going to get involved." She jumped up and shook her head. "I won't get involved. I mean it!" She walked out of the room and into hers, grabbed her coat and rushed out. Her life was in enough turmoil without bringing in Jill and

Addie's supposed problem.

A few minutes later Sheela looked up at the bleak, gray sky, then across the sodden grass of the park. Shoulders hunched and hands stuck deep in her jacket pockets, she walked past the empty swing sets and slide. Only a few others had ventured out on such a chilly, damp evening.

Later she dropped to a faded green bench and flung the end of her blue wool scarf across her shoulder. A dog barked and two cars drove past on the street. A man who reminded her of Aaron walked past her. She watched him until he was out of sight.

How did Aaron spend his Saturdays?

She frowned. She would not think about him.

"Sheela, you are a wonderful woman. You are special," he had said.

His words touched her again and she clung to them.

Chapter 10

ith an unhappy sigh Sheela unwound her scarf with icy hands as she walked across the lobby of her apartment building. After the crisp evening air the closed-in smells made her wrinkle her nose. Loud music blasted from Zelda's apartment. Sheela shook her head impatiently. Just as she reached the steps, Zelda's door burst open and she stormed out, shouting to Sheela.

Sheela turned around and waited, a shiver slipping down her spine. Had Zelda discovered Nadia?

Zelda flung out an arm. "Do I look like an answering machine? I don't like taking telephone messages for you."

Sheela stiffened. "What message?"

"I left it in your mailbox. I should've let you find it on your own, but I felt it was my duty to at least tell you about it." Zelda flung back her hair, turned and marched to her room, slamming the door.

Slowly Sheela walked to the row of gray boxes and opened hers. She braced herself in case it was from Wade or Bobby or Grandmother. Aaron's name and office number were scribbled on the paper and she sagged in relief.

"What could he want?"

She glanced toward Zelda's door and then over to the pay phone. She'd given that as her phone number to Aaron, but this was only the second time he'd ever used it.

"I wonder why he's at work so late, and on a Saturday night?" Quickly she dialed. He answered on the first ring and her legs almost gave way. She leaned against the wall. "Aaron, it's Sheela. I'm returning your call."

Glad lights danced in his eyes. He stood in her office with her phone at his ear. "Sheela! I'm glad to hear from you. I need the Procter file and I can't find it in your files."

"The Procter file?"

"I'm working on the account today so that I can talk to them first thing Monday." He wanted to ask her to come to the office just so he could see her, but he forced back the words.

"Did you look on your desk?"

"Yes. It wasn't there."

She closed her eyes and searched her brain. "How about my desk in the right hand drawer."

"I tried it. It's locked."

"No. It sticks sometimes. Try it again."

He leaned over and tugged, then tugged again. The drawer slid open and the Procter file lay on top of a pile of papers. He lifted it out and laughed. "You're right. I have it. Thanks."

"I'm sorry you couldn't find it. I had a couple of notes to type up for it before I filed it away." She hesitated. "I could come type them now."

"You could?"

"Yes." She waited, barely breathing.

"No. No, it's not necessary." Did disappointment sound in his voice?

"It wouldn't take me long at all."

"It can wait until Monday."

The sparkle left her eyes. "Are you sure?"

He tapped the file on her desk. He wanted to tell her to come. "I'm sure."

"See you Monday."

"Monday. Thanks, Sheela. You're a lifesaver."

She laughed breathlessly. "Hardly that."

"But you are! I searched the place for an hour!"

"Oh, I'm sorry!"

"It wasn't your fault. You had no way of knowing that I'd need it before Monday."

"I guess not. I went for a walk or I'd have called sooner."

He touched her pen, her pencil holder, her stapler. "Did you have a nice walk?"

She twisted her scarf around her hand. "It was cold."

"Winter's coming all right."

"Yes."

He had a million things he wanted to say to her, but he knew he shouldn't keep her. "I guess I'd better get to work. Go get warm and enjoy your evening."

"Thank you. Don't work too hard."

He laughed. "I usually do."

"I know."

"Bye, Sheela. See you Monday." Slowly, reluctantly he hung up, then sat at her desk, on her chair and held the file that she'd held yesterday.

She walked away from the phone with her purse

held tightly against her heart and his words singing in her head.

Sunday she slept in, woke past noon, dressed in old jeans with a warm pink sweater and reached for a box of corn flakes, then ate the granola instead. She fixed a cup of instant coffee, laced it with milk and sugar and drank it. The room was so quiet that she could hear herself chew. She knew By and Lillian were both in church but would be back soon. They always went and they usually asked her to go with them. She never did.

She glanced around the room. What could she do to make the day pass quickly so Monday and work and Aaron would come? She flushed and brushed a hand across her cheek.

What was Aaron doing today? It was his day to have dinner with his family. She knew that he always looked forward to family dinners. He'd said that all of them would be there for the first time in months.

Priscilla was his older sister and she had the same blond hair. She was a writer and she'd married a writer. Sheela leaned back in her chair and smiled as she remembered the times Priscilla had come to the office to weep on Aaron's shoulder when she'd first fallen in love with Lang. She thought he hadn't noticed her. Lang and Priscilla married a year and a half ago and now they had a baby girl. Aaron had brought a picture of Lori especially to show Sheela. He was almost as proud of Lori as Lang and Priscilla.

Tera was a year younger than Priscilla and was engaged to marry Bob Alton, a tall, red-haired lawyer. Sheela laughed as she remembered meeting Tera for the first time. Tera had walked into the office full of life and energy and had said, "Hi,

Sheela. I'm Tera. Another of the Brooks family. I've heard so much about you that I had to come meet you." Tera looked more like her mother than the others. She was a gymnastic instructor and owned her own studio. "Come any time you want to work out, Sheela."

She'd agreed to, but never had. She sipped her coffee with a faraway look in her eye.

Kirk was the youngest of the family. He was a history teacher at Hope College. He'd flirted with her when they had first met and she'd immediately lifted her icy shield against him. His latest girlfriend was Carrie Zeigler and Aaron had said a few weeks ago that he thought they might marry.

Sheela pictured all of them around the dining room table, talking and laughing and enjoying each other. How would it feel to belong to such a family?

"What am I doing?" She jumped up and paced the room in quick, agitated steps. What was happening to her? For years she'd held herself aloof from others and now suddenly she was thinking of herself with the Brooks family.

A knock at her door interrupted her anguished thoughts. She flung it open, expecting to see Lillian or By, but it was Grace Keeler. Sheela frowned. Mrs. Keeler never came to her door. "Yes?"

Grace Keeler peered through her thick glasses. Her blue eyes looked five times the normal size. "There's a woman outside that wants you."

"Who is it?"

"How should I know? I was coming in and she wanted to come in with me. Can you imagine? But I wouldn't let her. I did tell her that I'd let you know she wanted to see you. She said it was important."

"Thank you."

Grace Keeler waited. "Well, aren't you going down?"

"In a minute."

"She's standing out there waiting. And it's cold out."

"I'll go down."

Finally Mrs. Keeler turned and walked away, mumbling to herself.

Sheela ran down to find her grandmother standing outside the door, shivering with cold. She saw Sheela and called to her. Her breath hung in the air. With a strangled cry Sheela turned and ran back to her room and closed her door. Her breast rose and fell.

"Grandma," she whispered hoarsely.

Slowly she walked to her blue chair and huddled in it, her knees pulled to her chin. She would not speak to Grandmother today or any day. She would not feel sorry for her because she was cold and lonely and frightened about Bobby.

After a long time she heard a timid knock at the door and she jumped as if a bomb had exploded beside her.

"Sheela, it's me, dear. Lillian."

Sheela ran to the door and opened it. Lillian stood there holding a saucer with a slice of pumpkin pie in her hand.

"I thought you might like this, dear. By said it's the best he ever tasted and I wanted you to have a piece. You do like pumpkin pie, don't you, dear?"

Sheela managed a shaky smile as she took it. "Yes. Thank you, Lillian."

Lillian smoothed the skirt of her flowered dress and fingered the strand of beads at her throat. "I had only enough Cool Whip left to put on a dollop."

"It looks delicious. Thank you." She started to close the door, but Lillian held out her hand.

"Dear, I saw your grandmother a few minutes ago. I told her that I would speak to you for her. She said you . . . you wouldn't talk to her."

Sheela's face flamed. "I can't talk to her."

"*Can't*, dear?"

"You wouldn't understand. I'm sorry, but I don't want to talk about her."

"I know something terrible is hurting you, dear. Me and By have been praying for you."

"You have?"

"Of course, dear." Lillian patted Sheela's arm. "I wish you'd let us help you. I do think you should find a way to talk to your grandmother."

"No. No. I can't."

Lillian nodded. "I won't press it, dear."

"Thank you."

"Enjoy the pie."

Sheela thanked her again in a weak voice and closed the door and leaned against it, shaking so much that she almost dropped the pie. Just how much had Grandma told Lillian? Sheela gnawed her bottom lip. "Stay out of my life, Grandma!"

Slowly Sheela walked to the counter and set the saucer down. Her throat closed and she knew she couldn't eat the pie now. She walked across the room and looked out at the bleak, cold day. Was Grandma still standing outdoors in the cold?"

"I won't, won't talk to her," whispered Sheela. Her mind whirled with terrible memories from her past and she fought and struggled until once again they were pushed far enough back that she could survive.

Suddenly someone pounded on the door and it shook as if it would break. Sheela cried out, trembling violently.

"Open this door, Sheela!"

It was Wade. She tugged at the collar of her pink sweater.

"I'll stand here and yell and pound until you open

this door, Sheela Jenkins!"

She stumbled across the room and yanked the door wide. "Leave me alone, Wade!" She looked past him to find By and Lillian in the hall watching them. They looked frightened, but concerned and ready to help her.

Wade pushed past her and slammed the door. His round face was red and his eyes dark with anger. His overcoat hung open, showing the dark suit and white shirt underneath. "I saw Emma a few minutes ago and she said you wouldn't let her in."

"How did you get in?"

"I waited until someone was going out and I caught the door before it shut. Your grandma should've done that, but she said she wouldn't force herself on you ever again."

"Good for her." Sheela crossed her arms and glared at Wade. "You shouldn't force yourself on me either!"

"I'm no old lady that you can push around. I told Bobby you'd come with me to the hospital today, and, by George, you're going to!"

She backed away from him, suddenly frightened of his anger. He was short, overweight and in his fifties, but she knew she was no match for him. "Get out of here, Wade. It won't do you any good to try to take me to Bobby. I won't go. You must know why."

"Sure. You think you're too good for her now that you're on your own."

"What? You know the truth, Wade!" Her voice rose and suddenly she was shouting. "She beat me. Did you hear me, Wade? She beat me and I'll never forget or forgive her for it."

He shrugged it away. "She said she got a little too rough with you at times, but she says she's sorry for it. She loves you and she wants to see you real bad."

"No! Never!"

"She's not getting well as fast as she should and the doctor said it's because she's worrying over you." He shook his fist at her. "Over you!"

"I don't care!"

"I'll carry you there if I have to."

"You wouldn't dare!"

"Wouldn't I?" He stepped toward her and she shrieked and jumped away. "You are going with me."

She dodged around him and flung wide the door. Just as she stepped out, Wade grabbed her arm. She cried out in fear.

Lillian and By flew out Lillian's door, looking ready for battle.

"What's going on here?" asked By.

"Help me," whispered Sheela.

"She's going with me," said Wade. "Mind your own business."

"You turn Sheela loose," said By, his fists doubled. He danced forward on the balls of his feet.

"Right now!" cried Lillian, brandishing her yellow umbrella. "You let her go or I'll bop you over the head with this."

Sheela struggled, but Wade's hold was too tight. She kicked out at him, but missed.

"You're going to see your mother now, Sheela Jenkins! I promised her."

"I will not go!"

"I'll call the police," shouted By.

Lillian held the umbrella high. "You want this over your head?"

"It'll only take them a couple of minutes to get here," said By.

Wade swore and pushed Sheela away. She stumbled against By and he caught her and held her

with a strength that surprised her. Wade disappeared down the stairs.

Sheela pulled away from By and rubbed her sore
arm. "Thanks," she whispered.

"That was thrilling, dear." Lillian's eyes sparkled
with excitement.

"Very," said By dryly. "Care to tell us what that
was all about?"

Sheela shook her head. "I can't. I just can't."

"If you can't, you can't," said By.

"How did you like your pie, dear?"

Sheela laughed around the lump in her throat. "I
didn't eat it yet."

"Bring it over and we'll share tea," said By.

"Thanks, but I'd rather be alone right now."

"You're alone too much, dear. You need to be with
people more often. With us or with your fine young
man. You need somebody to protect you."

By turned on Lillian. "Just what do you think we
did today?"

Lillian giggled. "We did protect her, didn't we?
But what'll happen when you move to your condo?"

"You can both move with me."

Tears pricked Sheela's eyes and she blinked them
back. "I guess I do want that cup of tea."

"Good," said By.

"And friends," Sheela whispered.

"Friends," said By with a grin.

"Let me get my pie and my key and I'll be right
with you."

"We'll stand right here and wait for you, dear."

"We want to make sure that man doesn't sneak
back here," said By.

Sheela ran to her room and caught up her keys
and her pie and walked out to join By and Lillian.

Chapter 11

aron looked across the dinner table at his chattering sisters. Priscilla laughed as she touched the pearls that hung down on her red and white dress. Tera turned her head and her diamond earrings flashed the same bold colors in her flowered dress. Both girls had always known they were special, but Sheela had been surprised, unbelieving in fact, when he'd told her that she was. Somehow he had to help her get over her past so that she could move ahead with her life. He sighed, folded his orange linen napkin and pushed it under the edge of his china plate. He brushed a crumb off the sleeve of his gray wool suit.

He glanced again at Priscilla just as she turned away from Tera and leaned against her husband and whispered to him. Lang turned his head slightly and nuzzled her cheek.

Suddenly Aaron wanted a wife to sit beside him at

family dinners. He wanted her to lean aginst him and whisper secrets for his ears alone. The longing engulfed him, startling him.

On his left, Kirk laughed at something Tera said. Aaron glanced at him as he unbuttoned the top button of his shirt to reveal the strong column of his tanned neck. His gray eyes twinkled with mischief and a dimple appeared in his left cheek as he laughed again. He didn't seem to be missing Carrie, but then he wasn't ready to announce a coming marriage to her or to anyone. But Aaron knew it would be soon, probably right after Tera's in May.

A picture of Sheela flashed in Aaron's mind. What kind of wife would she be?

Abruptly he grabbed his glass and downed the last of the water. He caught his mother's eye as she lifted a fine brow in question. He was thankful she couldn't read his mind. All of them wanted him to take time away from his business and marry. He smiled at his mother and she smiled back before she turned her attention to what his dad was saying.

Taylor pushed his plate back and leaned an arm on the table. "Tomorrow on my show I have three women working with the abuse center here in town. They're going to tell ways we can spot child abuse, then what to do about it."

Aaron leaned forward, eager to learn all he could to help Sheela. "Is there much child abuse in our city?"

Taylor nodded. "There is. Dr. Drake in E.R. at Grace Memorial says he treats several physical abuse cases a week. The sad part is, he can't prove it and he has to send the child home with his parent."

Kirk ran a finger around his collar. "I've talked with a few of my college students who were abused children. They said it's hard to live a normal life even after they're away from their parents. They have scars and it's sad to see."

Priscilla caught Lang's hand and held it. "I can't imagine anyone beating his own child! We would never do that to baby Lori!"

A picture of Sheela as an adorable baby, then a little girl flashed across Aaron's mind and tears burned his eyes. How could anyone beat her the way Emma Hall had said Bobby had? A muscle in his jaw jumped as anger at Bobby rushed through him.

"An abused child carries bitterness and hatred and anger as a way of life." Taylor's hazel eyes were full of concern as he looked around at his family. "They don't know how to deal with the feelings and often the feelings cause the abused child to become a child abuser and at times a criminal. It's a problem that needs attention."

Nola smiled at her husband. "I think you're going to get an attack from some of the viewers, the ones who don't want to admit that abuse goes on in our society."

"You're right," said Taylor.

"I'm glad you're doing it anyway, Dad," said Tera.

Aaron thought about telling them about Sheela, but he held back, knowing Sheela would pull further into herself is she ever realized that he or his family knew about her past.

Later he slipped on a warm jacket and walked out the back door into the yard where he'd played as a boy. Once their home and property had been in the country, but slowly through the years, the city had crept out and around them. Their ten acres had kept close neighbors away.

A dog barked and a car honked. Aaron glanced up at the bleak gray sky and wished for sunshine. He hunched his shoulders against the chilly wind as he walked around the picnic table toward the bird house that he'd helped Kirk build several years ago.

"Sheela, Sheela. How can I help you?" He lifted his head as if he expected to see the solution, but deep in his heart he heard the answer; pray.

"Thank you, Heavenly Father.

"Right now I bind Satan's attack on Sheela in the name of Jesus. I set her free to find Christ. I set her free of bitterness and anger and hatred in the name of Jesus. I speak peace and love and forgiveness to her. I speak inner healing of all the scars that were made by her mother.

"I pray that the eyes of her understanding be opened so that she can receive Jesus in her life. I pray that laborers in the harvest will cross her path and witness Christ to her and any time I can, I will witness Christ also.

"I asked for a special understanding of Sheela and a special wisdom for dealing with her and a boldness to do what the Spirit leads me to do.

"Send help to Sheela's mother also so that she can find peace and comfort in Christ.

"Father, your Word says that anything I ask, believing, in Jesus' Name will be done. Thank you in advance for the answer. In Jesus' Name, Amen."

Aaron took a deep, steadying breath. "Thank you, Father God. You are the only answer for Sheela."

The back door banged shut and he turned to watch his mom walk out, wearing a gray wool coat and black boots. He strode toward her with a glad welcome.

"I was hoping you wouldn't want to be alone, Aaron."

A powerful love surged through him and he gathered her close and held her. She barely reached his chin. He smelled her perfume and a hint of her shampoo. "I love you, Mother. I thank God for you! You were and are a good mom."

"Thank you, Aaron." She stood on tiptoe and kissed his cold cheek. "You're a precious son." She studied him silently and he knew she had questions about his thoughts whirling around inside her head.

He smiled, caught her gloved hand and walked around the back yard with her. Finally he said, "I have to help her, Mom."

"Who, son?"

"Sheela."

"I thought so." Nola nodded.

He stopped and faced her. "She's so alone!"

"You'll find a way to help her. I know you. You're a good friend to her."

"Friend! Hardly that. She won't let me get even that close."

"Since when has that stopped Aaron Brooks?"

He grinned. "You know me so well, don't you?"

"Yes." Nola's cheeks were pink from the cold. "I'd like you to bring Sheela here the first chance you can. She needs to be around a loving family, and not be so alone."

"I don't think she'd come."

"We want to get to know her."

"She's afraid of close contact with anyone."

"Be gentle with her, Aaron. Be gentle and kind and patient."

"I will."

"Bring her for the next family day."

"Mother, you've said many times that family day is just for family."

"I know. Bring her."

"My concern does not mean I'm falling in love with her. You know that!"

Nola smiled. "I know."

"Mother," he said in a warning voice.

She squeezed his hand. "You'll know the right woman when the time is right."

Just then the back door opened and Mariette Golden walked out. Aaron stiffened.

"She is not the right one," said Nola so low that Aaron wondered if he'd heard correctly.

"And how do you know that?"

"I just know. I like her, but she's not the one." Nola stepped forward with a warm smile. "Hello, Mariette."

"Hello, Nola. Aaron." Mariette's hood fell back to reveal long blond hair as she smiled at Aaron. "I hope you don't mind that I came over. I called and your brother said it was all right."

Aaron kissed her cheek and smelled her delicate perfume. He liked Mariette, but she didn't send his pulse leaping the way she had when first they'd started dating. "You're just in time for a game of pool. Did Kirk tell you that?"

Mariette laughed. "He mentioned it. I came prepared to beat everyone."

"You usually do," said Nola, smiling as she patted Mariette's arm. "I'm going in. I'll put the coffee on. Want a cup?"

"Sounds good," said Aaron.

"I'd love a cup," said Mariette. She slipped her hand in Aaron's arm. "I do want a couple of minutes with Aaron alone first."

He heard the serious note in her voice, caught the look in her blue eyes and he wondered about it. He studied her face as she watched Nola walk back to the house. He knew something was troubling her.

What would he do if she asked if he was ready to talk about marriage? Panic seized him, but he managed to force it away.

She was quiet while they walked to the picnic bench. He brushed a few brown leaves off and they sat down. She slipped her hand down his arm and caught his hand and gripped it as if her life depended on it.

"What is it?" he asked softly.

She turned wide blue eyes on him and trembled. "Aaron, I want to ask you something. Something important."

He stiffened, suddenly afraid again. "Yes?"

She gripped his hand tighter. "Aaron, we've been going together for several months now."

"Yes?" His stomach felt like a block of ice.

"Aaron, I have to tell you something that might . . . might upset you . . . but I must do it."

"Please, Mariette! Just say it." His voice softened. "We've been friends long enough for you to know that you can say anything to me. Almost anything."

"You know that I've been praying about . . . us."

"Yes." Should he stop her so that he wouldn't have to hurt her by turning her down?

"Aaron, I . . . met a man."

"What?" That he hadn't expected.

Tears filled her eyes. "Don't be angry with me or hurt. Please. I love you and couldn't bear to hurt you."

The relief was so great that he laughed aloud. "I won't be angry. Or hurt. What about this man?"

"His name is Joe Dowling. I met him at the last business meeting I had in Phoenix. And I . . . like him."

"Like?"

"Well, maybe love." She leaned against Aaron. "I know we've had kind of an understanding, but Aaron, I met Joe and I found I wanted to know him better."

"How does he feel about you?"

"The same."

"I would never stand in your way. You and I have been good friends and we love each other and we had fun together, but we never did fall in love."

"I know. I guess I needed to hear you say it. I would never hurt you and you know it."

"I know."

"I'm going to Phoenix again tomorrow and will be gone for a while. I wanted you to know."

"Invite me to the wedding, will you?"

She jumped up and he stood with a laugh. She flung her arms around him and they held each other a long time.

"I want you to find a wife, Aaron. I want you to have someone so you won't be lonely."

"When I do I'll let you know."

"What about Sheela?"

He stiffened. "Sheela?"

"I've seen the way she looks at you."

Blood pounded in his ears. "You're mistaken."

"Oh?"

"You are."

She shrugged. "Maybe, but I don't think so."

"Let's get inside and find Kirk for that game."

"Run away, Aaron. But one of these days you won't want to." Mariette laughed and squeezed his hand. "You'll be running right to her."

"I'm sure Kirk is waiting for us."

She grinned at him as she tweeked his chin. "Running, Aaron?"

"Who's running? Let's go." He managed a laugh as he walked to the house with her.

Chapter 12

Sheela finished the business call just as Mrs. Turner with the greeting card account, the last client of the day, walked out of Aaron's office. Sheela smiled and stood. "Goodbye, Mrs. Turner. Have a nice evening."

"Thank you, my dear. I will." Mrs. Turner pushed her purse strap higher on her slender shoulder. "I'm so glad to see Indian Summer come that I'm going to enjoy a nice walk in the country with my husband."

"That sounds wonderful." Sheela knew she'd enjoy the walk home tonight. She had finally given in about driving the car on rainy or cold days, but insisted on walking the other days. She watched Mrs. Turner walk out, then covered her typewriter and filed away the last three folders.

Aaron's door opened and he walked out. His white shirt sleeves were cuffed up and his tie off. "Sheela, come look at these layouts and tell me what you think. There's just something missing and I can't put my finger on it." He saw the covered typewriter and glanced at his watch. "Oh, I didn't realize it was so late."

"It doesn't matter. I'll look at them." She walked to his office with him, proud that he'd asked her to check layouts with him. He'd said many times that she had a natural ability for advertising.

She stood beside him while he showed her what he'd done. She studied them carefully. "I like them just the way they are. They should sell a lot of greeting cards. Was Mrs. Turner pleased?"

"Yes, but she left the final decision to me." He leaned back on his desk and smiled at Sheela. She still looked as fresh as she had at the beginning of the day. "I missed you today."

"But I was here all day."

"I know, but I didn't get to talk to you more than five minutes all day long. Would you have dinner with me?"

Her eyes widened. "Dinner?"

"Please." Suddenly it was the most important thing in the world to him.

She opened her mouth to say no, but instead said, "Yes. I'd like that."

"Great! I'll be ready in a couple of minutes if you don't mind waiting."

Panic flicked over her. What had she agreed to? "Oh, Aaron. Forgive me, but . . . but I really can't go with you."

"Do you have other plans?"

"No."

He shrugged and grinned, but inside his heart raced in alarm. "It's too late now. You already said yes and you can't go back on your word."

She locked her fingers together in front of her.

"I . . . I really shouldn't go to dinner with you."

"It's already settled." He smiled right into her eyes and she couldn't argue further. "The boss is the boss, you know." He laughed. "I'll be ready in a minute."

She nodded and laughed with him. "But nothing elaborate, please. I'm not dressed."

"You look beautiful."

Her hand fluttered at her throat. Beautiful, he'd said. "I'll wait in my office."

"Fine." He smiled and watched her walk out, closing his door after her. He wanted to leap high and click his heels, but he lifted his face and whispered, "Thank you, Heavenly Father."

She walked to the bathroom, combed her hair and repaired her makeup. She looked closer at her reflection. Her eyes were shining! She frowned and turned quickly away.

At her closet she lifted out her coat, bag and purse. She turned off the soft background music automatically.

Why had he asked her for dinner? Many other times he'd gone through whole days without seeing her more than a few minutes. What was different now?

"Bobby," she whispered, her hand at her mouth. He wanted a chance to convince her to visit Bobby in the hospital! He hadn't asked her to dinner just to have time with her. He didn't do that kind of thing.

Sheela moaned, the hurt so deep it was a physical pain. She shot a look toward his closed door, then ran out of the office, closing the door with a gentle click. She leaned against the wall and changed from her heels into her walking shoes. Quickly she slung her bag over her shoulder and ran into the sunlight and the noisy rush hour traffic. She dodged a group of teenagers and ran toward home as if she were being pursued.

Back at the office Aaron whistled a lilting tune as he walked out of his office into Sheela's, knotting his tie in place. He stopped with a frown. "Sheela?" Was she in the bathroom? The door was ajar and he called her name again.

In a sudden panic he flung open her closet and found it empty. He tugged his tie loose and unbuttoned the top shirt button. "She left! She walked out on me!"

He strode across the room, shaking his head. He stopped to look out the window and blinked against the bright sun. "She walked out! But why?"

With a few long steps he reached the door and jerked it open. "I'll see why."

Angry and hurt, he ran to his car and drove to her apartment as fast as he could in the heavy traffic. "I'd better simmer down," he said hoarsely. Silently he prayed for the right words to say to her. At the curb he forced his pulse rate down, then ran to the front door. A tall man with a long black beard pushed the door open and Aaron caught it before it closed, and stepped quickly inside. Smells of hamburgers and garlic and cabbage blended together with stale cigarette smoke. Scraps of paper and dust balls filled a corner near the mailboxes. A baby cried and someone shouted, then blaring music drowned out the other noises. He scanned the mailboxes to find Sheela's number, found it and took the stairs two at a time. He knocked on her door, then knocked again harder.

"She isn't home, dear."

"She's at work."

Aaron turned to see a white-haired woman and a short, wiry man standing a few feet away. "Sheela's not home?"

The woman shook her head. "She never gets here

until five-twenty or so."

The man stepped forward, his hand out. "I know you're her boss, Aaron Brooks. I'm By Windfield and this is Lillian Ketchum"

"We're her friends," said Lillian, retying her apron as the men shook hands. "We're fixing supper and we were going to invite her to eat with us. She does sometimes."

"Would you like to join us tonight" asked By with a grin.

"Thanks, but I can't. I'm taking Sheela out for dinner tonight."

Lillian nudged By and they smiled at each other before Lillian turned back to Aaron. "Going to dinner together. That's nice, dear."

"She should be home any second. You're welcome to come to my place to wait for her," said By.

Aaron shook his head. "Thanks anyway. I think I'll wait near the door."

"You be very kind and patient with her or she'll run from you," said By.

"I know."

"She is afraid of people, dear."

"I'll be kind and gentle with her," said Aaron.

"You tell her we said to have a good time." By and Lillian said goodbye and By led her back to his room and closed the door.

Aaron looked down the dimly lit hallway and groaned. How he hated to think of her in such a place! Finally he turned and walked to the stairs. He'd wait for her all night if he had to. As he reached the middle of the stairs, he heard angry voices and he stopped and looked over the railing. Sheela and Wade stood below, glaring at each other. Aaron had never seen her so angry. Her dark hair was wind-blown, her cheeks red and her eyes shooting fire.

"I won't go, Wade!" Sheela stepped away from him. "You can't force me. I don't care how much Bobby begs you to get me, I won't go see her." Sheela trembled and clutched her bag to her.

Wade's face darkened and he grabbed Sheela's arm. "You're going with me. I promised Bobby." His breath came in short, ragged gasps as he tugged on Sheela.

A muscle jumped in Aaron's jaw and he clenched his fists.

"Let me go or I'll scream!"

"Who will care?"

Aaron jumped down the last three steps and faced them. "I will care. Let her go. Now!"

Sheela gasped, her face paled and her legs trembled. She hadn't expected to see him.

Wade glared at Aaron, but kept a firm hold on Sheela. "This is not your business, Mr. Brooks. I'm taking Sheela to Bobby and nobody will stop me."

Aaron blocked his way. "No, Wade. You will not take her against her will. You tell her mother that if Sheela wants to see her, she'll come by herself and won't be forced."

His words surprised her and she looked at him in gratitude.

Wade swore gruffly, pushed her away, and shook his huge fist at her. "Do you know how awful it is to see the pain on Bobby's face because you won't visit her? I made her a promise and I won't quit until I keep it!" He walked to the door, his head and shoulders pushed forward, but once again Aaron blocked his way.

"You will never, and I mean never, force Sheela to go with you. Or you'll have me to answer to."

Wade growled, ducked his head, and finally Aaron let him go.

Sheela sagged against the stairwell, her bag and purse on the floor beside her.

Aaron walked to her and pulled her to him. Trembling, she pushed her face against his neck and gripped the lapels of his jacket. He wrapped his arms around her and held her close, his cheek pressed against her soft hair. He smelled the delicate fragrance of her shampoo and a hint of perfume. "You're safe now," he whispered. "I'm here. You're safe."

Finally she lifted her face to him.

He saw pain in the depth of her eyes and he wanted to erase it completely. Gently he touched his lips to hers. She trembled and closed her eyes, accepting his kiss, savoring it, then hesitantly returned it. The world flipped upside down for her. He felt the kiss right to the soles of his feet.

He pulled away enough to look into her face. Her eyes were filled with wonder. He waited a fraction of a second to give her a chance to pull away. She didn't, and he took her lips again.

Her arms crept up around his neck and the kiss deepened. Her heart thudded against his and every nerve-end tingled with life.

He wanted the kiss to go on and the knowledge caught him off guard. He pulled away.

She stiffened, suddenly confused and embarrassed.

"I think we'd better go have our dinner." His voice was almost normal and he even managed a smile.

She jumped away from him, smoothing her hair. He had kissed her and she'd kissed him back. How could she face him now? "I . . . I can't go with . . . you."

"Yes, you can." He couldn't let her walk away now. "Please. I want you to. I made a reservation at

Steele's Steak House."

"No. No, I can't."

"Why?" He lifted a brow.

She flushed to the roots of her dark hair. "You're my boss and we. . . kissed."

"Yes, we did." He smiled. Somehow he had to get back on even footing with her. "And we'll both survive, I think."

She didn't know if she would.

He stepped closer to her. "Why did you run away from me earlier?"

She looked down at the dirty floor. "Now I know that I was very foolish. I didn't want you to talk to me about visiting Bobby."

"Is that it?" He almost shouted in relief. "I promise I won't even talk about your mother unless you want to. Now, will you go with me?"

She wanted to refuse, but she didn't have the strength. "All right. But I won't stay out late!"

"Do you turn into a pumpkin?"

A smile tugged at the corners of her wide mouth. "I might. And then what would you do?"

"I'd pick you up and carry you home. Then I'd sit and watch you until you turned back into yourself."

"I thought maybe you'd carve me into a jack-o'-lantern."

He shook his head and said very softly, "I'd never hurt you."

The words wound around her heart and warmed her totally. "Never?"

"Never. Never on purpose."

She smiled. "I suppose I could eat a steak."

"Me too. With a baked potato and a salad." He picked up her things and walked her to his car before she could change her mind.

A few minutes later she sat across a small table

from him with smells of steak strong around the dimly lit room. The waitress walked away with their order. Tables were full of other customers, laughing and eating and seeming to enjoy themselves. Silverware clinked on china plates. She watched a busboy load a cart with dirty dishes from a table beside them.

Aaron sipped his water and set it back in place. "Tera's wedding plans are coming right along. I'm going to be one of the groomsmen."

"Does she have her colors picked out?"

They talked about Tera and Aaron's family until the food arrived, the steaks and potatoes steaming.

During dinner Aaron asked her about several of the ad ideas they'd worked on and Sheela discussed them easily without crawling into her shell.

Back at her apartment he walked her to the outer door and unlocked it for her. He felt her stiffen and he knew she was afraid he would kiss her again. He stopped just inside the door and said, "I'll see you tomorrow morning, Sheela. Thanks for tonight."

She nodded, unable to meet his eyes. "Thank you for dinner. And . . . for rescuing me from Wade."

"Any time. Don't you think I make a great knight in shining armor?"

She laughed at that and finally could look at him. "Yes, yes, you do."

He ran his finger down her cheek and held it near the corner of her mouth for a minute. "Jesus loves you, Sheela." He smiled, turned and walked out.

She watched until he reached his car. "Jesus loves you, Sheela," rang in her ears and touched her heart.

Finally she walked alone to her lonely room, unlocked her door, but before she could step inside Lillian stuck her head out her door. She beamed when she saw Sheela.

"Did you have a nice time with your young man, dear?"

Sheela nodded. It would do no good to tell Lillian that Aaron wasn't her young man. "We had steak."

"And did you have a nice conversation, dear?"

"Yes. I'd better go in now."

"Oh, I forgot to tell you that Addie wants to see you. She said please stop in even if you get in late." Lillian wrinkled her brow. "I hope nothing's wrong with little Addie."

"Me too." Sheela dropped her shoes and bag in her room, but kept her keys. "Good night, Lillian. You tell By that I had a good evening."

"I will, dear. He'll want to know." Lillian lowered her voice. "He went out a while ago so Nadia could get a little fresh air."

Sheela smiled and hurried to Addie's apartment and knocked on the door.

"Who is it?" asked a tiny voice.

"It's me, Addie. Sheela Jenkins."

Addie opened the door wide and tugged Sheela inside. Addie's eyes were red from crying and her hair was in tangles.

Concerned, Sheela bent down to her. "What's wrong, Addie?"

Addie sniffed hard and wiped the back of her hand across her runny nose. "I got scared."

"Of what?"

"Being alone."

"Isn't your mom here?"

"No. She left me tonight, but she didn't have enough money to pay Mrs. Ketchum and you weren't home, so she said I was big enough to stay alone. But I got so scared and I wanted you."

Sheela's heart swelled with compassion and she pulled Addie close and held her. Why hadn't Jill stayed home tonight? Addie was much too young to stay alone for any length of time. "You're all right now. I'm here." Aaron's words echoed in her mind and she smiled. "I'll stay here until she comes."

"But she'll get mad at me for telling you I was alone."

"I'll handle it. Don't you worry."

Trustingly Addie looked up at her. "I love you, Sheela."

"Oh, Addie. I love you!"

"Want to see a picture I drew?"

"Yes."

Addie led Sheela to the kitchen table and showed her the drawing of a horse and rider. They sat side by side as Sheela studied the picture. "Some day I want to have a horse and ride like the wind just like in the book I'm reading. Did you ever have a horse when you were a little girl?"

"Never. I've never even been on a horse. Once I touched one."

Addie laughed. "I touched one once too, but I never rode one. Mom has. She said it's fun. This new guy she's going with, Mike's his name, lives on a farm and he has a horse. That's where she is tonight."

"Did she say when she'd be back?"

"She didn't know, but she said it wouldn't be late. But look!" Addie pointed to the clock on the stove. "It's almost eight and she's not back yet."

Echoes of Sheela's childhood came to her and she knew just how Addie was feeling. "Are you worried that she'll never come back?" Sheela reached for Addie's hand and held it.

Addie nodded.

"She'd never leave you, Addie. She loves you."

"Are you sure?"

"She said so."

"But she might decide I'm such a big bother that she'll go away with some guy and leave me all to myself."

"She won't do that."

"But I'm scared."

"If she did, I'd take you for my little girl."

"Oh, Sheela! Would you?"

"Yes."

"And you wouldn't leave me or . . . or anything."

"Or what?"

Addie looked down at the table. "Nothing."

Sheela wanted to press for an answer, but couldn't find the courage. "Let's get you ready for bed. I'll fix your bath water and shampoo your hair and comb it for you."

Addie jumped up with a glad cry and ran for the bedroom. Her room was so tiny it was cramped with a single bed, a dresser and a cardboard box that held a few toys. The bathroom separated Addie's room from Jill's.

Later after her bath Addie sat on the floor in front of Sheela on the couch while Sheela carefully combed her wet hair. "Did you have a date tonight, Sheela?"

Sheela flushed. "Not a date exactly. I had dinner with Aaron Brooks."

"Oh, he's so nice!"

"He is."

"Did he kiss you?"

Sheela blushed to the roots of her hair. She gripped the yellow comb tighter and worked harder on Addie's hair. "I wonder if I'll ever get this knot out of your hair!"

"I wish you'd always do my hair. Mom pulls it a lot. But she does know how to fix it pretty for me for school most of the time. If we have time."

Sheela breathed a sigh of relief that Addie dropped the question about the kiss. She didn't want to think about Aaron's kisses. But once again she felt his mouth covering hers and her heart raced just as it had then. Impatiently she pushed the feeling and the thoughts away.

At nine she tucked Addie into bed. "You smell clean and you look like a little angel." Sheela lifted a fluffy yellow cat out of the toy box and tucked it under the blanket beside Addie. "I'll be right in the other room if you need me, Addie. Sleep tight."

"I will. Good night, Sheela."

"Night." Sheela turned to go, but Addie jumped up on her bed and hugged her hard around the neck. Sheela hugged Addie back as if she'd never let her go. Finally she tucked her back in and walked out, leaving her door ajar.

Sheela curled on the couch with the ragged, but clean afghan over her. The room looked the same as hers except Jill had a few pictures of landscapes hung on the wall. The smell of bath soap and shampoo was still strong in the room. A bright bouquet of red plastic roses stood in a vase on the TV set. A rush of water whooshed through the pipes. Sheela leaned her head back and closed her eyes. Suddenly she was with Aaron again and she remembered every word, every gesture he'd made. Thoughts of his kisses warmed her, but she shook her head and refused to dwell on them.

About ten-thirty Jill walked in, tears streaming down her face. She stopped short when she saw Sheela and tried to wipe her face dry with the sleeve of her sweater. "Hey, what're you doing here?"

Sheela dropped the afghan in place and stood, pity for Jill taking over the anger she'd felt earlier.

"I came to watch Addie. I came to see her and she

was alone, so I decided to stay with her until you got home. I figured you'd have asked me if I had been home when you left."

Jill nodded and sank to the chair beside the end table. "Oh, Sheela, my life is so messed up!"

Sheela perched on the edge of the couch. "Why?"

"Do you know how old I am?"

"No."

"Twenty-five. Twenty-five going on fifty!"

The same words from Bobby echoed in Sheela's head and she locked her hands in her lap.

"Hey, I can't make anything of myself! I have to support me and Addie. I get so frustrated sometimes I could scream!" Jill flipped back her hair. Her eyes were haunted and her face haggard. "I have no life of my own. Do you know that if it weren't for Addie I could've stayed with Mike tonight? But no, I had to come back. He'll never call me again. I know he won't."

Sheela studied Jill for several seconds. "You could give Addie up . . . for adoption."

"What? No way! I love my little girl! I'm just saying it's not fair!"

Oh, how many times had Bobby said the same thing? Sheela crossed her legs and smoothed her skirt over her knees. "Just what do you want out of life, Jill?"

Jill flung out her arms. "A man, a home, a happy life for me and Addie. Is that too much to ask?"

Sheela pushed back the panic at the same words that she'd heard Bobby say many times.

"You don't understand at all, do you, Sheela?" Jill jumped up and paced the room. "You got a good job. You could probably have any man you want. You don't have a kid holding you down. A kid that needs shoes and jeans and lunch money. It's hard.

Hey, it's been hard for ten years! When I was sixteen I was already a mother. What were you doing? Going to school and thinking about the prom, right?"

She hadn't been thinking about the prom, but she understood what Jill was saying. "You shouldn't have become pregnant."

Jill laughed hysterically. "It's easy for you to say! And don't you think I didn't think of it when it was too late?"

"Can't you get some kind of government assistance?"

"Welfare, you mean?"

"Yes."

"No way! Hey, I don't want that kind of life!" She kicked off her shoes and walked to the kitchen. "Want a cup of tea?"

Sheela glanced at the clock. "I have to get up early."

"Me too."

"I guess I could take time for one cup." Sheela sat at the kitchen table while Jill fixed the tea. To her surprise she was beginning to understand Jill's feelings. Was it possible that she could understand Bobby if she tried?

Jill kept up a constant chatter about her evening with Mike and what a disaster it had turned into. Finally she sat down across from Sheela and lifted her steaming cup to her gloss-free lips. "You're a good listener, Sheela. I need to pour out my feelings to someone so I don't do something I'll be sorry for. I have this . . . this problem."

Sheela stirred her tea without looking up. She could feel the silence that Jill had left for her to ask about the problem, but she couldn't do it.

"Sometimes I'm a little rougher on Addie than I

should be." Again Jill waited, but Sheela couldn't ask.

"That's why I go out so much. I need time to myself. I need somebody to take care of *me* for once." Jill brushed away a tear. "Life is rotten. You ever think so, Sheela?"

"Yes. Yes, I do."

"I wish I could find help. Hey, did you ever ask your boss about help for me?"

"I'm sorry, but I forgot. But I will. I know that he'd tell you that Jesus loves you and wants to help you." Sheela didn't know what else to say. She sipped her tea and for a long time sat in silence.

Jill sniffed and dabbed her eyes. "You're a good friend, Sheela."

Sheela smiled hesitantly. Was she really?

"I was ready to give up tonight, but you were here and listened. Thanks."

Sheela nodded. "I'm glad I could help." And she meant it.

Chapter 13

heela lifted her face to the warm Indian Summer sun as she stood on the small footbridge at the park. Aaron had given her two hours off for lunch today and she'd decided to spend it in the park. It was a beautiful day for the second day of November. Fluffy white clouds dotted a bright blue sky.

A man and woman walked past arm in arm. They stopped, kissed and walked on. Sheela flushed and looked quickly away, her fingers on her burning lips. Yesterday Aaron had kissed her, but today he'd acted as if nothing had happened between them. She'd been ready to freeze him out if he became too personal with her, but he hadn't.

She gripped her shoulder bag tighter. Her navy blue suit jacket and skirt were almost too warm for comfort. Wood chips crunched under her walking shoes.

Just what had his kisses meant?

She shook her head, unable to imagine. He couldn't be in love with her. Nobody could love her except Addie because she was lonely and needed someone.

Jill needed someone too. Sheela sighed. If Jill had a better paying job, she and Addie could move into a nicer place and that would help push away the depression she felt at times. Addie needed a regular baby-sitter, a younger one who could keep up with her and who could watch her day or night. Sheela nodded. Maybe later today she'd ask Aaron if he could find a way to help Jill and Addie.

"Oh, Aaron, why did you kiss me?" She shot a look around to make sure no one had heard her sudden outburst, but she stood alone on the bridge.

Slowly Sheela walked back onto the regular sidewalk. A small black dog ran toward several pigeons pecking in the dirt in front of a bench. The pigeons fluttered into the air and the dog stood looking up, barking wildly, shuting off the sounds of traffic for a while.

A blond woman and a tall dark man pushing a baby carriage walked toward Sheela. She glanced toward them, then looked again. It was Priscilla and Lang with baby Lori.

"Hello," Sheela said stiffly.

"Sheela! It's wonderful to see you!" Priscilla impulsively hugged Sheela, startling her and cracking her reserve. "Lang, you remember Sheela, Aaron's secretary. And Sheela, look at baby Lori."

Lang shook hands with Sheela and smiled. "Beautiful day, isn't it? We couldn't stay cooped up any longer."

"I know how you feel," said Sheela. She peeked in the carriage to see the baby cooing and smiling.

"How she's grown! She's beautiful!"

"We think so," said Priscilla, beaming. "We brought a picnic lunch with us. Please join us, Sheela."

"Yes, do," said Lang.

Sheela stepped back a step. "Oh, I don't know."

"We'll tell you all about the book we're writing today," said Lang with a laugh and a twinkle in his dark eyes. He tugged his black sweat shirt down over his faded jeans. "I'm sure you'd want to hang on every word."

Sheela laughed. "I would like to hear about your book. I am an avid mystery buff."

"So are we," said Priscilla. She glanced around. "Let's sit over there at the table in the sun."

"I have an apple and a sandwich in my bag," said Sheela.

"Add it to our stuff and we'll call it potluck." Priscilla patted the bag she carried. "We're starving. How about you?"

Sheela shrugged.

Lang tugged a strand of Priscilla's blond hair. "Let's eat now while Lori is contented."

A few minutes later Sheela sat across the picnic table from Priscilla and Lang with the small lunch on a red checkered cloth in front of them. Priscilla described in detail Lori's ability to smile and coo and turn over.

"You'd think by listening to her that we have the smartest baby in the world," said Lang with a wink at Sheela.

"And we do!"

"I think you must," said Sheela with a chuckle. "Tell me about your book."

Lang and Priscilla talked about it while they ate. Sheela told them of a few of her favorite mysteries and discovered that they'd met one of the authors that she preferred.

Just then Lori whimpered and Priscilla jumped up to lift her out of the carriage. She wore a soft pink sweater and bonnet with pink tights and tiny pink booties. Priscilla kissed her and held her out to Sheela. "Would you like to hold her, Sheela?"

"Oh, I might drop her!"

"No. Look. Hold one hand under her bottom and the other at her neck. See? Like this."

Sheela finally nodded and held out her hands for the baby. "She's so soft," whispered Sheela as she looked down at the tiny face. "And so beautiful!" The little nose was perfect and her eyes were wide and dark. She waved a tiny fist and cooed.

"You hold her like a pro," said Lang.

"I do?"

Just then Aaron walked up unnoticed and the picture Sheela made holding Lori took his breath away. He'd called Priscilla and Lang for lunch and learned that they were at the park, but he hadn't expected to see Sheela. His heart beat faster under his crisp white shirt. He wanted to scoop both Sheela and Lori into his arms.

Something made Sheela look up and her eyes locked with Aaron's and her pulse leaped. She watched him as he studied her and the baby. She could tell he liked what he saw and it pleased her more than she cared to admit.

"Aaron!" cried Priscilla, breaking the spell between the two. "What a surprise! Come join us. We still have a little left. How wonderful to have both you and Sheela with us!"

Lori squirmed and whimpered and Sheela flushed, suddenly embarrassed. "Maybe you'd better take Lori, Priscilla."

"I will." Aaron bent down and gently lifted Lori from Sheela's arms.

Sheela smelled his after-shave and her stomach tightened. His hand brushed hers, sending a tingling all over her.

Aaron sat beside Sheela and kissed Lori's tiny cheek. She smelled like baby powder. "Hello, precious. Uncle Aaron loves you."

Sheela's heart raced just watching Aaron with Lori.

"We were telling Sheela about our book," said Lang as he set down his can of soda.

"How's it coming?" asked Aaron. He balanced Lori in one arm as he reached for a sandwich with the other. He was aware of Sheela beside him and he wondered if he could eat or listen to Lang when all he wanted to do was talk to Sheela.

"It's super, but right now we need to do a little research." Lang slipped an arm around Priscilla.

She smiled at him before she turned back to Aaron and Sheela. "Since we have Tera to give us help on gymnastics we're using that as a background. The story's about a woman gymnast at the Olympics who meets a Russian gymnast and they fall in love. They marry and then she learns that he had planned to defect.

"She thinks he married her only to give him his freedom and she's heartbroken.

"It's full of intrigue and romance and danger, but we need more help with what goes on at the Olympics from a gymnast's viewpoint."

Sheela leaned forward eagerly. "I have a friend who was a gymnast in the Olympics. By Windfield. I know he'd talk to you. He lives in my building."

"Great! Set up a meeting, would you, Sheela?" asked Lang.

"Of course. Tomorrow?"

"Tomorrow's perfect," said Priscilla.

Lori burst into a loud wail and Aaron quickly passed her over to Lang. He gave her a pacifier and she stopped crying and snuggled against him.

"I think our picnic is over." Priscilla gathered up her things and Sheela jumped up to help. "Don't let me rush you, Aaron."

He bit off a piece of apple. "No problem," he said around the bite.

"I'll get back to the office," said Sheela. "Thanks for lunch."

"Wait. I'll go with you." Aaron pulled his long legs out from under the table and stood up. No way would he pass up an opportunity to walk in the park with Sheela!

She gripped her bag tighter as he kissed Priscilla and Lori and shook hands with Lang.

"See you later," he said as he grabbed up his jacket that he'd dropped on the bench.

"I'll call you with the meeting time with By," said Sheela over her shoulder. She stumbled and Aaron caught her by the arm. She jerked away and he looked at her questioningly, then smiled. She looked away, unable to speak.

In silence they walked across the park. He stopped at the street. "Did you drive?"

"No."

"I didn't either." He tugged his tie loose, held his jacket by the collar and flipped it over his shoulder. "It's warm, isn't it?"

"Yes." She walked beside him toward the office.

"Lori's a little doll, isn't she?"

"Yes."

"Don said his wife is getting very impatient."

A truck rattled past and she waited until the noise

faded. "I'm surprised the baby didn't come yet since the doctor said it could be any day."

"Don is really frazzled. I talked to Roxie this morning and I know she's just as bad."

"They're both tired of waiting."

"Mom says the baby shower next week will help. It's funny, isn't it?"

"What?"

"Waiting for a baby. It's hard to imagine how it'd be."

"Yes." She didn't want him to ask her if she ever wanted a baby. She didn't want to tell him that she'd never have children because she might treat them just as Bobby had treated her.

A jogger ran around them, heading toward the park.

"Could I ask you something, Aaron?"

"Anything." Just walking beside her was a satisfying experience and it surprised him.

"Do you remember meeting Addie the other day? The little girl."

"Sure."

"Her mother is having a tough time of it. She's raising Addie alone on the money she gets from working at the Copper Door. She needs help with Addie and she won't get it from Welfare."

"Good for her!"

"I would like you to talk to her sometime and see what you can do for her." Sheela glanced at him and quickly away. "I told her you'd tell her that Jesus loves her and wants to help her."

Aaron nodded as pride in Sheela washed over him in waves that left him weak in the knees. "I'll do that for sure. When can I talk to her?"

They crossed the street at the green light. "She's working dinner shift at the Copper Door. How about seeing her there?"

"We could have dinner together and both of us talk to her."

At the sight of a short, hefty man several feet away she cried, "Oh, no!"

"What?"

"It's Wade again! Just outside the office. Won't he ever give up?"

"I'll talk to him." His face set, Aaron was silent until he stood beside Wade. "You will not speak to Sheela unless she wants you to. Understand?"

Wade's round face turned brick red, but he looked away from Aaron to Sheela. "Bobby goes home tomorrow, Sheela. She said you'd want to know."

"Well, I don't!" Sheela inched around Wade and Aaron and ran inside to the safety of her office. She patted perspiration off her face with a tissue. "Why can't he leave me alone?" She jumped when Aaron walked in.

"Sheela, I'm sorry your wonderful lunch break was spoiled by that."

"I wish he'd leave me alone!"

Aaron leaned against her desk and watched her walk to her chair. "One of these days you'll want to talk to Bobby and get this all settled between the two of you."

She shot a look at him. "Get what settled?"

He chose his words carefully so that she wouldn't know that he knew about the beatings. This was not the time to tell her. "You can't live happily until you settle the fight between the two of you."

"Then I'll have to be unhappy."

"Oh, Sheela."

She lifted her chin. "You promised not to bring Bobby up to me."

He nodded. "You're right. But I will not stand by

and do nothing when I see how sad you are."

She bit her lower lip and looked down at her locked fingers in her lap.

"What's the answer about dinner at the Copper Door? How about right after work?"

"I can't." Would she if she could? Her heart raced and she couldn't find the answer. "I told Lillian that I'd get home to take Addie. Lillian gets very tired if Addie's with her too long at a time."

"We could take Addie with us."

"But then Jill wouldn't talk freely."

"You're right."

The phone rang and Sheela answered it immediately. When she heard Mariette Golden's musical voice a dark cloud enveloped her. "It's for you, Aaron. Mariette Golden."

"Oh!" With a happy smile he reached for her receiver and she let him take it. "Mariette! How are you?"

Sheela walked to the bathroom and closed the door with a bang. How could Aaron kiss her one minute and talk so sticky sweet to Mariette the next?

Sheela's reflection bounced back at her and she saw her flashing eyes and her flushed face. "You can't trust anyone!" she hissed under her breath. "Not even Aaron Brooks!"

Finally she regained control of her emotions and walked back to her office to hear Aaron say, "I love you too, Mariette. See you when you get back. Bye." He hung up, but stayed on her desk, a faraway look on his face. Sheela cleared her throat and he glanced up and smiled.

"I just had a brilliant idea, Sheela."

"Oh, did you? And just what is it?" She knew her voice was icy, and she hoped he noticed.

"We could have dessert later. After Jill gets home

to take Addie." He watched her pull further into herself and saw the lines of hostility in her body by her stance.

She flipped back her dark hair and her nostrils flared. "No! Never!"

"Sheela?"

"I do not want to be friends with you or have dinner with you or even have dessert with you! We must get back to a business relationship only!"

Her words struck him to the heart. He clenched his fists at his sides. "Can't you let anyone close to you?"

"Meaning you?"

"Yes!"

"No!"

He felt as if he'd been punched in the stomach. "Then I suggest we both get to work. This is an office and we do have work to do." He strode to his office and slammed the door.

She sank in her chair and stared at the plants hanging at the window. Slowly tears filled her eyes, then gushed down her cheeks and she ran to the bathroom for privacy.

Blood pounding in his ears, Aaron paced the room. The harsh, angry words seemed to fill the room. Over and over he played the conversation with Sheela, first angry at her words, then struggling to understand her.

He sat at his desk, but couldn't work. With his elbows on his desk he propped his chin in his hands. "God, help me," he whispered.

Slowly his anger faded away, but the sharp words between himself and Sheela hung over him like a black shroud. He knew he had to apologize even if she didn't.

"Help me, Father God," he whispered.

He took a deep, steadying breath, slipped on his jacket, straightened his tie and walked the few steps, that suddenly felt like miles, to his door. He looked out at Sheela bent over her typewriter. The blue fabric of her suit hugged her slender shoulders and back. Her face was pale and her eyes red-rimmed as if she'd been crying.

"Sheela?" His voice was low, but she heard and lifted her head. He saw the pain in her eyes before she masked it with icy reserve. He walked to her desk and looked down at her. "Sheela, forgive me."

She bit her lower lip, fighting against the urge to fly into his arms.

"Please. I should not have snapped at you."

Her anger melted, but the hurt remained and she couldn't answer.

"I am so sorry."

She saw that he meant it and a tiny crack appeared in her armor.

"I never wanted to hurt you. Only help."

Tears pricked her eyes, but she wouldn't let them fall.

"I hadn't realized that I was forcing you into a friendship with me."

"Don't." She shook her head slightly to stop him from saying more. "I am sorry, too. I over-reacted."

"I'll be more careful in the future." He knew he'd have to walk softly or she would disappear from his life and he didn't want that to happen.

"I will try to keep my personal life from interrupting my work here."

"Don't worry about it." He smiled down at her, and she finally managed a tiny smile back.

Chapter 14

e was out of the office more than he was in for the next two weeks and she breathed easier. Yet his casual attitude hurt and puzzled her and left her more lonesome than she'd ever been. Their conversations, the special attention he showed her, had come to mean more to her than she had realized. For the last several days when he talked to her it was about business except when he told about his meeting with Jill. That meeting hadn't accomplished anything because Jill was too engrossed in a man she'd just met. Sheela glanced at Aaron's door. He was in the office working with Don on the Chow Down Dog Food account.

The phone rang and she jumped and answered it.

"Don't hang up, Shee. It's me."

"Bobby!" Sheela's throat closed and her mouth went dry. "Why are you calling?"

"To talk to you. To see you. I'm home and you

haven't come."

"And I won't either." Sheela shivered. "I'm sure Wade told you."

"But I want you." Bobby's voice cracked and a sob escaped. "I miss you, Sheela. Please come see me. You'd only have to stay a minute. Please."

Sheela's hand trembled. "No, Bobby. We have nothing to say to each other."

"But we do! We got a lot of catching up to do."

"I have work to do."

"Please don't hate me! Please don't! We got to forget the past. I've suffered enough for what I did to you. Don't make me suffer more."

Sheela dropped the receiver in place with a clatter, then covered her face with her hands. How could Bobby suggest that she forget the past?

"I'll never beat you again," Bobby had said at least once a week during her teen years. "I'll think of another way to punish you, but I won't beat you."

But the beatings had continued until finally when she was nineteen and almost out of business school she'd left with a vow that she would never return, nor see Bobby again.

Sheela rubbed her arm that had been broken twice by Bobby. Deep down the bone still seemed to hurt, but she knew that it was only the awful memory.

"Anything wrong, Sheela?" Aaron had walked in quietly, then stopped when he saw her anguish. He wanted to go to her and pull her close, but he'd worked very hard to keep his distance so she wouldn't run from him.

She looked up in alarm. "I didn't hear you come in."

He pushed his hand into his pocket and fingered his keys. "What's wrong?"

"Nothing I can't handle."

Should he leave it at that? For some reason, he couldn't. His plans to keep his distance evaporated. "Wade?"

"No."

"Your mother?"

She nodded.

He sat on the edge of her desk. She was in pain and he couldn't walk away. "I'm sorry. If there's anything I can do, tell me."

"There's nothing," she whispered.

"There is something you can do for me."

"What?"

He'd toyed with the idea, but suddenly he knew it was a great plan. "Come for Thanksgiving dinner next week. Priscilla and Lang want to tell you how much By Windfield helped them. Lori wants to show you how she can do the push-ups. I want a Thanksgiving dinner with my own special guest so I won't feel so left out when the others all have someone. So, will you come?"

"What about Mariette?"

"I want *you* as my guest. Will you come?"

He wanted her! "I'll think about it."

He grinned. "I'm going to take that as a yes."

"No!"

"You mean you won't come?"

"No. I didn't mean that." She brushed back her dark hair. She dreaded Thanksgiving day since she'd learned that By and Lillian would be out for the day. And Jill and Addie would be away for a long weekend.

"My family would love having you there."

"I don't know if I should."

"I won't eat you for dessert."

She laughed just as the phone rang. She grabbed it up to keep from further conversation with Aaron.

"I won't take no for an answer," he whispered.

She turned away from him. "Hello." She sounded very breathless.

"Sheela, it's Nola Brooks."

"Oh, Mrs. Brooks! Aaron is right here."

"No. Wait. Please. I'd like to speak to you first. Do you have a minute?"

Sheela caught her upper lip between white, sharp teeth. "Yes."

"I would like you to come for Thanksgiving dinner next week. Will you?"

"Thanksgiving dinner?" She glanced back at Aaron and he bobbed his brows and grinned. "Aaron just now asked the same thing."

Aaron laughed and leaned close to the phone. "Hello, Mother. She's coming for Thanksgiving."

"No!"

"What?" asked Nola.

Aaron gently tapped a finger on Sheela's nose. "You are going to our house for Thanksgiving dinner. Please?"

Sheela rolled her eyes and couldn't resist a minute longer. "Yes."

"What?" asked Nola.

"Mrs. Brooks, I'll be glad to have Thanksgiving dinner with you. Is there anything I can bring?"

"Just yourself. Don't dress up. We're very casual on Thanksgiving."

Sheela said goodbye and hung up.

Aaron caught her hand and lifted her up to twirl her about the room. "This is a glad day for me."

Sheela's cheeks turned pink and she tried to push away from him. "Please, don't."

He dropped her hands and stepped back, but his eyes sparkled and he grinned. "I'm glad you said yes."

"Me too."

"I'll pick you up about ten-thirty next Thursday. Write it on your calendar."

She nodded, but she knew the day and the time were already written on her heart. Maybe she'd regret it later, but after two weeks without special attention from him she couldn't refuse such a marvelous opportunity to be with him.

Thanksgiving morning she was dressed and waiting by ten. She opened the box on the couch and looked inside at her new dress. It lay in soft peach folds and she knew it looked great on her. She'd talked to Priscilla who said Sheela should take a dress in case they all decided to go out for dessert later.

What would Aaron think of her dress?

Her cheeks flaming, she closed the box and picked up the bag that held her shoes and makeup. She walked downstairs just before ten-thirty to find him walking up to the door. He wore jeans and a large red and black sweater with a black shirt under it. Her heart leaped and she wanted to fly to meet him. Suddenly she turned, ready to run back to her room and safety, but she knew it was too late. She had promised to go to his family dinner and she intended to keep that promise.

When she opened the door, he smiled and took her bag. "We're going to have a beautiful day, Sheela."

"I am nervous about being with your whole family."

"Don't be. You'll fit right in." He walked with her to the car. "Wait until you taste Mom's dressing! And Tera's fruit salad."

As the seat belt clicked around her, Sheela wondered if she'd be able to eat.

Later, at his home, they started toward the front door when another car pulled in behind Aaron's.

"It's Kirk. And Carrie. Let's go say hello." Aaron touched his hand on the back of her waist and walked with her to Kirk's car.

Kirk and Carrie slipped out of the car and Aaron introduced Sheela to Carrie. Sheela saw the pride in his eyes when he looked at her and it startled and surprised her.

"Hello, Carrie."

"Hi." Carrie looked like a college girl in her jeans and sweater instead of the dean's secretary. She was almost as tall as Kirk and her hair was long and dark. "I'm glad to meet you, Sheela. Are you still in college?"

"No."

"She's my secretary," said Aaron.

"Lucky Aaron," said Kirk and Carrie jabbed his arm. "And lucky me. We have the two most beautiful girls right here in our yard, Aaron. What more could we ask for?" He chuckled and leaned close to Carrie. "Except maybe Mom's home-cooked Thanksgiving dinner."

"Oh, you," said Carrie as she flung her arms around his neck and kissed him. "Now isn't that a lot better than turkey and dressing?"

"I don't know," said Kirk. "Let me see again."

"Let's get out of here, Sheela," said Aaron with a laugh. "These love birds need privacy. We'll go see the rest of the family."

Sheela wanted to turn and run, but she walked to the wide front door.

In the house she talked to Tera and her future husband, Bob, held Lori and asked Priscilla and Lang about their book. Aaron took her to the kitchen to talk to his parents and help them finish with dinner.

At the groaning table, aromas drifting up and around the room, Sheela bowed her head with the others while Taylor prayed over the food. Aaron reached over, squeezing her hand and whispered, "Thanks for coming."

She nodded and smiled back.

She listened and talked and ate and smiled more than she ever had. The turkey was tender and juicy, the dressing perfect with the right amount of spices to suit her. Creamy mashed potatoes, an apple salad and corn along with pickles and olives rounded off the delicious meal. A tiny slice of pumpkin pie with a dollop of real whipping cream filled the very last bit of her stomach and she leaned back with a satisfied sigh.

"Mr. Brooks," Carrie said during a lull in conversation.

"Yes."

"I watched your show a few weeks ago on child abuse."

Sheela tensed and Aaron bit back a gasp of alarm.

"How about if I start to clear the table?" asked Aaron.

"Aaron," said Taylor, shaking his head. "Carrie isn't finished."

Aaron tried to send a message to his dad, but he was turned to Carrie and didn't catch it.

Carrie leaned forward earnestly. "It was done very well and it made me aware of my own neglect. I joined the child abuse center and I've been helping twice a week."

"That's wonderful, Carrie," said Kirk.

"In one case the child seemed determined to protect his parent even though he was in physical danger. Isn't that cowardly on the child's part?"

Sheela locked her icy hands in her lap and the

blood drained from her face. "Maybe the child feels guilty for turning in his parent," she said sharply.

"But why should he?" asked Carrie with a frown.

"There are extenuating circumstances," said Aaron. He wanted to rescue Sheela, but he didn't know how without causing a scene that would humiliate her.

"That's right. There are," said Sheela in a low voice.

Carrie shook her head. "No. I think any child who takes a beating time after time is asking for it. Asking for attention any way he can get it. I say if he can't turn in his parent, then he deserves what he gets!"

"Carrie!" barked Aaron and she blinked in surprise.

The room spun and Sheela pushed back her chair in the sudden silence. She almost fell, but Aaron caught her arm and helped her from the room and led her to a quiet den.

Sheela leaned against a chair back, breathing in great gasps of air.

"Sit down," said Aaron softly. "Please." He urged her to the couch and he sat beside her.

Giant tears rolled down her face.

"You're safe, Sheela." He pulled her close and held her. "I'm here with you. No one will hurt you."

Awkwardly she clung to him, sobbing raggedly.

"Shh. Sheela. Shh." Aaron stroked her back and hair.

"She doesn't know what she's talking about," whispered Sheela.

"I know."

"No, you don't understand."

"Tell me then."

"She's wrong."

"Tell me, Sheela."

She looked into his eyes and her face crumpled. She gasped, "I can't! It's too awful!"

"Tell me anyway." He caressed her soft cheek. "Please."

"Bobby . . . Bobby beat me. I wanted to get away from her, but I couldn't. And I couldn't turn her in to the police or anybody. She's my mother!" Her last words ended on a wail.

He rocked her gently in his arms. "I know. I know."

Between sobs and words of encouragement from him she told him about her years with Bobby. "Do you understand? Really?"

"Yes."

"How I hated her even when I loved her!"

"You are a wonderful, special girl, Sheela, and God loves you."

"Nobody loves me!"

"God loves you, Sheela Jenkins. He wants you to know that. He wants to be your father and your strength and your protection."

"I am so alone!"

"Jesus loves you. Once you accept Him into your life you'll never be alone again."

The words slipped into her heart and suddenly she knew she wanted Jesus now without delay. "Please, please, I want Him in my life. I need Him!"

"We'll pray right now." Aaron leaned his face against Sheela's. "Heavenly Father, thank you for your great love for Sheela. Jesus, right now she is opening her heart to you. Receive her as yours to-day. Give her a new heart this day and make her whole."

Sheela listened to his prayer with tears running down her cheeks, wetting his face too. "I give myself to you, Jesus," she whispered brokenly. As she prayed, a huge weight lifted off her and disappeared. A light exploded inside her and she smiled through her tears.

"You're God's child now, Sheela," said Aaron, brushing the dampness from his eyes., He pulled a tissue from a box on the coffee table and wiped her tears. "You, Sheela Jenkins, are a new person in Christ!"

"Yes, I am!" Her face glowed as she gripped his hands. "I came to your house for dinner and received a miracle."

"Praise God."

"Praise God," she whispered.

He pulled her close again and held her against his leaping heart.

Finally she pulled away. "I embarrassed myself in front of your family by running out that way. What will they think of me?"

"They'll be delighted about your news. We've all been praying for you."

"Thank you." Hastily she brushed away fresh tears.

"Let's go tell them right now before they burst with curiosity."

She nodded, but hung back. "I don't know if I can face them."

"You're not alone now, Sheela. You belong to the great family of God and His entire family is with you to help you." He cupped her face in his hand. "And I'm with you, too."

She took a deep, steadying breath. "Let's go."

And when she told them they clustered around her, taking turns hugging her until she felt as if she was floating on a high colored balloon.

Aaron stood to the side and watched, his arms folded and a smile on his lips.

Sheela turned from Taylor to speak to Aaron, but

he wasn't there. A sudden panic gripped her and frantically she looked arond the room until she saw him beside the fireplace. Her panic vanished and she smiled.

He stayed at her side as they talked and played for the next few hours.

"Who's ready to change clothes and go get coffee?" asked Tera, standing arm and arm with Bob after a game of Ping-Pong.

"And dessert," said Bob.

You children go ahead," said Taylor. "Your mother and I will watch Lori and relax together."

Aaron whispered in Sheela's ear, "You will go, won't you?"

She nodded.

"Good."

Priscilla motioned to her and she ran upstairs with Priscilla and Tera to change in their old bedroom. In the dressing room she slipped on the soft peach dress and circled her slender waist with the leather belt. She brushed her dark hair back from her face and held it back with wide peach-colored combs. A simple gold chain with a tiny heart hanging from it rested on her breast. She slipped into her black leather heels, brushed on eye shadow, mascara, and blush, smoothed on lip gloss and was ready.

Carrie stopped her in the bedroom. "Sheela, I love your dress!"

"Thank you. I like yours too. That shade of green makes your eyes look almost black."

"Thanks." Carrie pushed back her dark hair. "Sheela, I'm sorry for upsetting you so much a while ago."

"It's all right now."

"You feel very strongly about child abuse, don't you?"

Sheela nodded and waited for the panic to swamp her, but it didn't.

"You're probably doing everything you can to help abused children, aren't you? I know I'm planning to do more. And I am going to try to see the child's viewpoint after this, not just my own." Carrie picked up her purse off a chair. "I think we'd better get down to the guys. Pris and Tera are waiting for us."

Sheela pressed her hand to her fluttering stomach and walked with Tera, Carrie and Priscilla to join the men.

Aaron stood at the front window, looking out at the lawn. He had changed into a dark suit with a striped tie. He turned at the sound of the women coming. A light leaped in his eyes when he saw Sheela walking toward him. He'd always known she was beautiful, but now there was a special glow about her that came from the inside. "You look gorgeous!" he whispered hoarsely.

"Thank you. So do you." Trembling with pleasure at the sight of him, she slipped her hand through his arm and together they followed the others to the cars.

Chapter 15

nce again dressed in jeans, Sheela curled up in her blue chair holding the Bible that Aaron had just given her. As they stood in the lobby to say goodbye, he'd pulled the Bible from his pocket.

"This is my Bible that I've marked Scriptures in, the one I study from. I want you to have it, Sheela."

"But I can't take it, Aaron."

"I'll use one of my other Bibles. I can re-mark Scriptures. I want you to have this one. Please. I know you'll treasure it as much as I do."

"I can get a Bible of my own, Aaron."

"Sheela, will you please let me do this for you?"

She took it and held it to her thankfully. He smiled and said softly, "I'll see you in the morning."

She smiled dreamily. Soft music played from her cassette player. Smells of Thanksgiving dinners still hung in the building heavy enough to drift into her room. By and Lillian had gone out. She knew they'd be at her door when they returned to ask about her day with the Brooks family. She laughed. Oh, wouldn't they love her news? They would be pleased that finally she'd opened her heart to God.

She rubbed the covers of the Bible and turned to First John three where Aaron had put his book marker. The very first verse leaped out at her. *See how very much our Heavenly Father loves us, for He allows us to be called His children—think of it—and we really are! But since most people don't know God, naturally they don't understand that we are His children.*

Tears welled up in her eyes. She was now God's child and He knew it! He called her His child and He was Love itself, Aaron had said. It was almost too much to take in.

Aaron had said, "Now that you're a child of God, the Holy Spirit has opened your spiritual eyes to see the hidden treasures of God. He'll reveal His truths to you as you study."

She read until someone knocked on her door. She jumped up and opened the door to see By with Nadia in his arms. For once his face was long and there was no twinkle in his gray eyes. The news she started to tell him died in her throat.

"What's wrong, By?"

He walked in and sank to the edge of her couch. Nadia stretched and curled up beside By. "I can move into my condo in two weeks."

"But that's wonderful! Isn't it?"

He shook his head. "How can I leave you and Lillian?"

"We'll miss you. Especially Lillian since you two spend so much time together." A thought popped into Sheela's head and she laughed softly. "You don't have to leave Lillian."

"What?"

"You could marry her. As for me I could visit you both often."

"Marry Lillian?" By gripped his knees.

"Yes. You care for her and she cares for you."

"I never thought of marriage at my age!"

Sheela leaned forward. "Never?"

"Well, maybe, but I don't think Lillian wants to marry a short, old gymnast like me."

"You could ask her."

He paced the room, his hands locked behind his back. Suddenly he stopped, his face red and dotted with perspiration. "I've never been married."

"You're a brave man, By, and I know you could find the courage to be a married man."

He thought about that for a long time and finally nodded. "You're right. Let's go talk to Lillian."

Sheela shook her head with a laugh. "You're kidding! She wouldn't want me there when you propose marriage to her."

"But how can I do it on my own?"

"You're brave, By. You've always been brave."

Before he could move someone knocked. "Probably Lillian," whispered Sheela, grinning. She opened the door to find Lillian standing there in her flowered dress and fluffy yellow slippers on her small feet. Her white hair waved back from her lined face and she looked from By to Sheela questioningly.

"What's going on here?" she asked suspiciously. "Are you two keeping secrets from me?"

By tugged Lillian into the room. "Sheela just came up with a great solution for us so I don't have to leave you behind in this place."

Sheela tried to catch By's eye and stop him, but he was looking intently at Lillian.

"She says we should get married!" By beamed proudly at Lillian, but she backed away, shaking her head.

"I don't get married to solve a problem," said Lillian stiffly.

By looked uncertain. "She said since we care for each other it'd be smart to get married."

"And who says I care enough for you to marry you, Byron Windfield?"

He stared at her and turned to Sheela indignantly. "Now, look what happened!"

"How could you embarrass me like this, Sheela? I thought we were friends." Lillian blinked away tears and marched out of the room.

Sheela fell back a step. "Oh, dear." Lillian's words stung her and she felt helpless all at once. "I hurt her."

By caught her hand and held it. "Don't take it so hard. She still loves you. It's me she hates."

"No! She can't hate you. I think you should've talked to her in private about marriage. Let her know you love her and want to marry her, not just because I suggested it, but because you want to."

"Well, I don't know if I want to."

"Are you going to get upset with me too, By?"

"No. No, I'm just mad that Lillian didn't like the idea of marrying me."

Sheela sat beside Nadia and stroked her. "Maybe if you sent her flowers and courted her she'd change her mind."

By rubbed a hand over his balding head. "I only have two weeks."

"Work fast, By."

He shrugged. "I'll give it some thought."

"And prayer."

"Yes. That, too. Come, Nadia. Let's go home." He bent down and she jumped lightly into his arms.

Sheela peeked into the hall to make sure the coast

was clear. The hall was empty so she opened the door wide and By walked out and down to his room.

Slowly she changed into her pajamas, brushed her teeth, cleaned her face and climbed into bed. She pulled the blanket to her chin and smiled. A whole new life stretched before her. Quietly she talked to her Heavenly Father just as she'd heard Aaron do.

The next morning she drove to work as rain mixed with snow hit the windshield. The office was locked and she knew she was the first to arrive. She smiled at the thought of seeing Aaron. The first thing she saw was a white note propped next to her phone. She picked it up, butterflies fluttering in her stomach. Aaron's strong, bold handwriting leaped out at her.

"Sheela, I was called out of town on the dog food account. I'll be back as soon as possible, but I'll call Monday. Keep loving Jesus."

It was signed "A."

She sank to her chair and her shoulders slumped. Could she survive without seeing him? "Oh, Aaron."

The door burst open and Don flew in. "Sheela! Is he in?"

Sheela jumped up. "No. Is something wrong?"

"Roxie started labor and we're sure it's the real thing. I came to get some work to take back with me. But I have to see Aaron."

"He's gone for a few days. He said he'd be calling Monday. But I have a number where I could reach him if you want me to call."

Don stabbed his fingers through his already spiked hair. "I guess I could go with what I have for Larkins, but I wanted Aaron's okay first."

"Sorry."

"How about you looking at it, Sheela? I know Aaron trusts your judgment."

Sheela followed Don to his office and looked over the colored brochure for the Olds dealership. "Maybe this should be here instead."

"You're right."

"But I like the rest of it. I'm sure Aaron would too."

"Good. I'll finish it and get it to the printers." He glanced at his watch. "A baby, Sheela. Can you beat that? We've waited all these months and now we're going to see the little guy."

"That's wonderful, Don. Is there anything I can help you with so you can get right back to Roxie?"

"I need the Barber Account and I think you'd better get me Mason's Account. Who knows when I'll be back."

"You know Aaron wouldn't want you worrying about work at this exciting time."

"I know, but we have deadlines for them and I never miss a deadline if I can help it."

"You're a good man, Don. I know Aaron appreciates you."

"Thanks." He dropped a folder in his briefcase. "I'm going to be there for the delivery, Sheela. It's frightening, but exciting. A baby! My own baby!"

"Here, Don." She slipped the layout into the folder and handed it to him.

"I should be able to think straight later. Thanks, Sheela."

She nodded and hurried to pull the other files he needed. She sent him out the door. "Be sure to call when you have news, Don."

"I will. I'll write it in the sky!" He laughed and ran across the hall to the heavy glass doors.

The silence surrounded her, but soon she was busy answering the phone, rescheduling Aaron's appointments, answering mail and filing. Just before she locked the door for the evening the phone rang again. It was Don, almost too excited to speak.

"It's a boy!"

"Congratulations!"

"He's beautiful and we named him Nathan Alexander and he weighed eight pounds and five ounces. Roxie's great. Proud of Nathan. Tell Aaron when he calls."

"I will. Tell Roxie I'll be up to see her tomorrow or Sunday."

"She'll like that. See you later."

She hung up, smiling, then dialed the florist and sent flowers to Roxie in Aaron's name. The long wait was over.

Would Roxie or Don ever abuse baby Nathan? She shook her head at the dreadful thought. It was unthinkable.

Yet she knew that many of the babies born today would be abused. Carrie had asked her what she was doing to help abused children and she hadn't answered. Sheela bit her lip. She'd help by breaking the terrible cycle in her family. She'd never have babies. It was a great tragedy that she would learn to live with. For now she was happy for Roxie and Don.

Monday morning Sheela walked into the quiet office with a spring in her step. Today Aaron was calling. She hung her coat in the closet and changed into her navy blue heels. The rain and snow had stopped last night and this morning the sun shone brightly, but she'd driven to work to get there faster.

The phone rang and she ran to it, answering in as businesslike a voice as she could manage.

"Hello, Sheela. How are you?"

At the sound of Aaron's voice, her nerve ends tingled and butterflies fluttered wildly in her stomach. Weakly she sank to her chair and closed her eyes. "Aaron. I'm fine."

He sat on the edge of his motel bed and gripped the receiver tighter. A longing to see her welled up inside him until he couldn't bear it. "Anything new?" How calm and collected he sounded!

"Roxie had a boy!"

"Hey, that's great! Send her flowers."

"I did. I knew you'd want me to."

"You did?"

"Yes."

"Thanks. Anything else?"

She leaned back in her chair and smiled dreamily. "I rescheduled your appointments without any problems."

"Thanks. I knew you'd handle it well."

She twisted a strand of dark hair around her finger. "How're you doing with the dog food account?"

"I've been getting the TV commercials finished. I think you'll like them."

"I'm sure I will."

"I might be able to get home tomorrow."

Her head snapped up. "Great!" Did she sound too enthusiastic?

He leaned back on his pillow. "It feels like I haven't seen you in weeks."

"I know."

He wanted to ask if she missed him as much as he missed her, but instead he said, "How's the weather there?"

"Nice today. It was snowy and rainy over the weekend. How about there?"

"Sunny and warm. You wouldn't think it was the end of November." He twisted the phone cord. "Have you been reading the Bible?"

"Oh yes! I love reading the verses you marked!

Sometimes I have to read them over and over to really know what they're saying, but I've learned that I am the righteousness of God in Christ and that God's love is shed abroad in my heart by the Holy Spirit."

He smiled at her enthusiasm and sat up, leaning forward with his arms resting on his legs. "Have you read that you are a new creature in Christ? Your old self is gone and God put a new spirit, a recreated spirit in its place. You are created in God's image. The old Sheela Jenkins is dead. The new Sheela Jenkins has God's nature and God's ability and love."

"How can that be, Aaron?"

"It just is. It's a miracle of rebirth. When you accepted Jesus Christ as your personal Savior, you were born again. You are now a new Sheela. All the old patterns are broken."

Tears filled her eyes. "Does it mean that . . . that the child-beater pattern is broken too?"

"Yes. With God in you, it is. As you study the Bible and see God as He is, you'll grow to be more and more like Him. You are free from your past. Jesus set you free to be like Him."

Tears of gratitude filled her eyes as the full impact of what he said hit her. "Oh, Aaron, it's too good to be true!"

"But it's true."

"Thank you! Thank you for praying for me and helping me find God!"

"My pleasure. I want the very best for you always, Sheela." He glanced at his watch and scowled. "Oh, Sheela, I just noticed the time. I have an appointment in a few minutes. I hate to say goodbye, but I must. See you soon."

"Soon," she breathed, brushing at her tears.

"Goodbye, Sheela."

"Bye, Aaron."

Oh, he hated to hang up! "See you soon." He dropped the receiver in place and sat with his head in his hands. "Sheela, Sheela. How can I live without you?"

Sheela dabbed fresh tears from her eyes and rubbed the receiver as if she could touch Aaron through it. "I miss you, Aaron. I love you."

She gasped at the sound of her words. Love? "I do! I love him!" In her heart she knew that she'd loved him for a long time, but she could never admit it even to herself.

"I love him," she whispered in awe. It took her breath away and she couldn't move.

Chapter 16

he ran into the office, shaking snowflakes from her coat. She'd seen Aaron's car in his spot and knew he was in his office. Soon she'd see his dear face and hear the sound of his voice.

Was it possible that he loved her?

She had struggled with the question for hours. At times she thought it was possible and at other times she knew it was preposterous. Maybe when she saw his face and the look in his eyes when he saw her, she'd know.

She hung up her coat, changed from her boots to her black heels and tried to force her heartbeat back to normal. She tugged her gray skirt in place and combed her shoulder-length dark hair. Her legs trembled and she clutched the back of her chair for support. Shivers of excitement ran up and down her spine as she walked to the connecting door. she touched the door and it swung slowly in. She started to take a step, then froze. The color drained from her face.

Aaron and Mariette stood near his desk, locked in an embrace.

Sheela backed away, then turned and ran, great sobs tearing at her throat. She fled from the office without her coat or her purse, fled from the building into the snow, fled from the embrace that had shattered her life. Cold wind whipped her hair and jacket, but she didn't feel them. Slush seeped through her shoes, turning her feet wet and cold. About a block from her office she stopped in a daze and looked around to see where she was. People walked past, looking at her strangely. She lowered her head, her cheeks flaming, and walked back toward the office. She would get her things and go home and never see Aaron again. She'd move away from her apartment, away from the trouble between Lillian and By, between Addie and Jill. Somehow she'd find the courage to get another job and forget about Aaron.

Just outside the building she stopped, suddenly afraid to walk in. Hands gripped her arms and she gasped and turned her head to find Wade there.

"This time you're going with me," he said grimly.

"No! Let me go this instant!" She struggled, but his strength was too great for her.

"I told Bobby I'd bring you, and by George, I will!" He pushed her toward the car at the curb. One of her shoes fell off, but he wouldn't stop to get it. He shoved her into the back seat of the car on the driver's side, slid in himself and roared away.

She grabbed at him and screamed, "Let me out!"

"You trying to kill us? Sit down and relax! You're going to talk to Bobby and then I'll take you back."

Sheela slumped back and crossed her arms. She

felt like the helpless little abused girl again. "I won't talk to her."

"Oh, yes, you will!"

"I won't!"

"You're not leaving until you do." He stepped on the gas and roared down a narrow street and pulled to a stop in front of a small house. "Bobby's been waiting long enough for you, Sheela Jenkins. You're going to talk to her and that's final."

Sheela pressed her lips tightly together and shook her head. He hauled her from the car and her foot froze as she stepped into a pile of slush. He pushed her ahead of him through the front door. The heat of the room surrounded her, leaving her weak. Smells of coffee and burned toast turned her stomach.

Bobby looked up from a game show on TV and quickly clicked it off with her remote control. She wore a flowered robe and her hair was once again bright red and fluffy. "Sheela! Oh, Wade, you brought her! Come here, baby, and sit by my side. I can't get around easily."

Sheela hung back, but Wade pushed her forward. She stumbled and her shoe fell off. She half fell in the corner of the faded couch. She struggled to stand. "He forced me to come, Bobby! Is that the way you want it?"

Her face clouded over. "I want it any way I can get it, Shee." Bobby turned to Wade. "Thank you, honey. Now, you sit over there and let me and Sheela catch up with each other."

"I want to leave now," said Sheela sharply.

"Not till Bobby's done with you," snapped Wade.

Sheela knew Wade blocked her escape and once again she was forced to sit in the same room with Bobby just as she'd had to do all her growing-up years. Nothing had changed. But deep inside she felt a stirring and she remembered that she'd changed. She was no longer alone. Silently she prayed for help.

"Talk to me, Sheela," said Bobby with a bleak smile. "I've been waiting so long. Talk to me."

"If I don't, will you beat me?"

"Don't!" Bobby covered her face with her hands and sobbed.

Wade struggled up with a roar. His plaid flannel shirt hung over his dark green twill pants. "Don't you dare hurt her more than you already did, Sheela!"

Sheela gasped. "Me hurt her? She hurt me. All of my life!"

"And I'm sorry for it," whispered Bobby.

Sheela turned on her and cried, "You always were!"

"But this time I mean it."

Sheela bit her lip and looked straight ahead at the TV stand.

Finally Bobby dried her tears and smiled weakly. "Please, Sheela, tell me about yourself."

"I have nothing to say."

"Don't be that way."

"What do you expect?"

Bobby pressed her fingers to her mouth.

"You're a monster, Bobby!" Sheela jumped up, her fists clenched. "You can't keep me here against my will!"

"She can't, but I can," said Wade gruffly.

Sheela sank weakly in the corner of the couch, feeling helpless and lost.

In his office Aaron walked Mariette to the door. "I'm glad about your move, Mariette. I know you'll be very happy in Phoenix with Joe."

"Thank you, Aaron. I couldn't leave without telling you goodbye. Let's keep in touch."

"We will." He kissed her again and she walked out. He looked around Sheela's empty office. It wasn't like her to be late. "Hurry, Sheela. I've been waiting too long for you."

He sat back in her chair with his hands locked behind his head, his dark jacket flapping open to reveal his crisp white shirt and paisley tie, and his eyes glued to the door. It seemed as if he'd waited his entire life for her and now he didn't want to lose her.

He wanted to marry her.

He laughed aloud. "Yes. I want to marry her!" For years his parents had prayed for his wife, and the last few years he had, too. He'd prayed that he would know when he saw her, and he did. "I want to marry you, Sheela Jenkins, and I want to spend the rest of my life with you. Will you have me?"

Could he ask her the all-important question when he saw her? Or would she freeze him out with one of her looks?

The phone rang and he answered it, expecting to hear her voice, but it was Mrs. Turner about her contract. He answered her question quickly and hung up with a frown. Sheela had never been late to work that he could remember.

He glanced toward her closet and saw the door slightly ajar. Slowly he walked to it and looked inside to find her coat, walking shoes and purse. "She's already here," he said, puzzled. Where had she gone? He checked the bathroom and Don's office, then looked out in the corridor. Voices drifted toward him. He glanced toward the outer door and then strode toward it, his stomach a ball of ice.

Snow swirled in the air and cold wind blew against him as he stepped outdoors. Why would she be outdoors without her coat? He started to turn back when he saw a black high-heeled shoe at the edge of the sidewalk. He picked it up. It looked like Sheela's shoe. Could it be?

He thought of Wade and his attempts to grab Sheela. "That's it! It has to be!"

He ran back inside. He might've jumped to the wrong conclusion, but he had to check it out. He'd call Bobby to see if Sheela was with her. With an unsteady hand he called information for Bobby's phone number. None was listed and he dropped the receiver in place. "Heavenly Father, right now in the name of Jesus help me find Sheela. Keep her safe."

He forced his hand to stay steady as he quickly rang Sheela's apartment. Zelda answered on the tenth ring, her voice sharp with anger. He asked her about Sheela and she snapped that Sheela wasn't home, that she knew because she'd just been upstairs. She hung up before he could ask anything more.

"I must find Bobby and Wade and I'll probably find Sheela. I'm sure of it." He tugged at his tie and unbuttoned his top button. How could he get Bobby's address?

"The hospital!" He dialed them only to have them refuse to give the address to him. He slammed down the receiver, silently crying out for wisdom from God.

"Dad! He can get it!" He dialed his dad and waited until he could be found on the set. "Dad, I need a favor."

"Anything, Aaron. What is it?"

"I must have someone's address. The hospital has it, but won't give it to me. Use your influence to get it. Barbara Jenkins. I need it now, Dad!"

"I'll call you right back. Later I want to know what's going on."

"Yes. Later." He hung up only to have the phone ring again. He watched the phone like a hawk its prey. Finally, after three phone calls from business associates, his dad was on the line.

"1825 Apple Street, Son."

"Thanks, Dad." Aaron dropped the receiver in place and ran for the door, locking it after him.

In his car he pulled out the map of the city and found Apple Street. Perspiration dotted his upper lip and forehead. If Sheela wasn't with Bobby, where could she be?

Several minutes later he found 1825 Apple Street and parked at the curb. He took a deep breath and slowly let it out. "Help me, Father."

He ran to the door and knocked, then waited. He couldn't just burst in if she wasn't there.

Inside the house Sheela jerked around, staring at the door. Maybe now she'd be able to get away.

"Get rid of whoever it is, Wade," said Bobby. "Me and Sheela aren't finished."

Sheela jumped up. "I am."

"Sit down!" barked Wade and she sat.

He jerked open the door, saw Aaron and tried to slam the door in his face.

"You have her, don't you?" Aaron pushed his way in and saw Sheela near the tattered couch.

"Aaron!" Was he an illusion?

Bobby gasped.

"Sheela, are you all right?"

She ran to him and flung herself into his arms. "Oh, Aaron. You came for me."

He held her to him and felt her heart hammering against his. He glared at Wade. "You brought her against her will! How could you treat her that way?" He turned to Bobby. "How could you? Her own mother!"

"Mr. Brooks," said Bobby weakly as she pushed herself up. She stuck her crutch under her arm and hobbled across the room. "I only wanted to see my baby. Don't blame Wade. And don't blame me. I love her!"

"You have a strange way of showing it," snapped Aaron.

Bobby stood before him, her eyes wide with anguish. "Don't take her away from me. Not yet."

"You don't deserve to have her for your daughter, but it's Sheela's decision to stay or go." Aaron looked into Sheela's face. "Sheela?"

"I want to leave now. Take me out of here now. Please." She clung to him and he held her tighter.

"We're leaving," said Aaron coldly. He walked her toward the door. "Sheela will come see you when she's ready, Mrs. Jenkins. Not before."

Bobby burst into tears and Wade circled her slender waist with his thick arm. "Don't go, Sheela!"

Bobby's anguished cry softened Sheela's heart, but she hardened it and walked out with Aaron and he slammed the door, cutting off Bobby's wails.

"Your feet! They're bare!" Aaron scooped Sheela up in his arms and walked to his car.

"Oh, Aaron. I'm so glad you found me. I was so frightened! I didn't think I'd ever get away from them."

He set her in the passenger seat and closed the door, then ran to slip in under the steering wheel. He lifted her hand to his chest and held it. "You're safe now, Sheela."

"Safe!"

"I will not take you to your apartment and leave you there! We'll go to the office." Reluctantly he released her hand, started the car and pulled away from the curb.

She told him in great detail about Wade abducting her, her voice quivering when she mentioned Bobby's obsession. "How could she think I'd want to talk to her and tell her about my life?"

"You're her daughter. She says she loves you." He carried her inside, set her on the desk and slipped her walking shoes on her icy feet.

She looked down at his dear head as he bent over her. "I didn't think you'd come for me."

"I was frantic when I couldn't find you."

She thought of Mariette in his arms and whispered, "You were?"

He gripped her hands and held them as he looked into her eyes. "How did Wade manage to grab you without my hearing him?"

Sheela trembled. "I ran ... outdoors and he ... grabbed me."

"Outdoors without a coat?"

She ducked her head and a tear slipped down her cheek.

"What is it, Sheela?" Gently he lifted her face with his finger and thumb under her chin.

"Don't. Please."

"Tell me what upset you."

"I saw you. And ... her."

"Who?"

"Mariette." Just saying her name sent a fresh wave of pain crashing over Sheela.

"And?"

"Nothing."

"Just what did you see?"

"I saw her in your arms."

"And that made you run?"

She nodded.

He held her face between his hands. "I was saying goodbye to her. She's going to Phoenix to marry Joe

Dowling."

"She is?"

"Yes."

"Don't you care?"

"I'm happy for her." He lifted Sheela down and wrapped her in his arms.

She looked into his eyes in wonder.

"Sheela, I love you."

"Oh!"

"I love you." He bent his head and kissed her with all the built-up passion that he'd denied so long.

She clung to him and returned his kiss with a passion that matched his.

Finally he lifted his head. "I love you."

"Oh, Aaron, Aaron. I love you!"

"Do you know what that does to my heart?" He caressed her flushed check and smiled. "Sheela, my precious sweetheart, will you marry me?"

With shining eyes she nodded and he pulled her close again.

Chapter 17

aron ran his finger down her cheek to her chin, leaving a trail of sparks. The love he felt for her was greater than anything he'd ever imagined. "I think a Christmas wedding would be perfect, don't you?"

"Christmas? In three weeks?" Suddenly frightened again, Sheela pulled back from him and bumped against her desk. "But that's so soon!"

He reached for her, but she ducked around her desk, using it as a shield between them. He frowned. Was he losing her again? "We'll make it April, then. Is that better?"

Before Sheela could answer, the door opened and By and Lillian burst in with Nadia. Snowflakes clung to their coats and hair.

"We had to come, dear." Lillian looked ready to cry.

Sheela rushed to her side and took her arm. Since

Thanksgiving Lillian had avoided her and Sheela was glad that she was finally speaking to her again. She'd told both of them about her salvation and Lillian had been happy and almost forgiving. By had been overjoyed.

"Come sit down. And tell me what happened," Sheela urged.

Anger flashed from By. "Zelda found Nadia." He stroked the long white hair on his cat's back.

"Oh, no!" cried Sheela.

"She did," said Lillian, nodding.

By sagged against the desk. "She was sneaking around and spying on me from Old Pop Bottle Bottom's room and caught me with Nadia. She pounced on me, shrieking at the top of her lungs that she knew all along that I was the one with the cat. She called a friend of hers to come get Nadia and take her to the pound. She said she wouldn't even give me a chance to find a home for her."

"We snuck out and came to you, dear."

Aaron folded his arms and watched Sheela with her friends. Finally when he could find the chance he asked, "What's this about your cat?"

Together they told him and he smiled and spread his hands. "I have a solution for you."

"What?" cried By and Lillian together.

Sheela smiled proudly at Aaron from where she stood beside Lillian's chair. Leave it to him to have an answer.

Aaron patted Nadia's great white head. "If you want, I could keep Nadia at my place until you're ready to move into your condo."

"Oh, Aaron," said Sheela, love shining from her eyes.

"That's nice of you, dear."

"I might not go," said By.

"What?" cried Lillian and Sheela together.

"I can't leave you two behind."

"Oh, By," whispered Lillian with a catch in her voice.

Aaron pulled Sheela to his side. "Sheela is going to marry me soon, so you don't need to worry about her."

"Wonderful!" By beamed with pleasure. Suddenly he turned to Lillian. "And you're going to marry me. These two found each other and so did we."

Lillian blushed. "We did?"

Sheela rested her head against Aaron and with a grin watched her friends.

By shook his finger at Lillian. "We care about each other and we're going to get married right away and move into my condo."

Lillian looked helplessly at Sheela and she nodded.

"I won't take no for an answer, Lillian Ketchum!"

"All right," said Lillian. "We'll get married."

By set Nadia on the carpet and pulled Lillian up close and hugged her and she blushed even brighter.

"I'm so happy for you two," said Sheela, dabbing sudden tears from her eyes.

Nadia mewed and rubbed against the desk leg.

Aaron pulled his keys out of his pocket. They jangled as he twisted off a big gold one. "Here's the key to my place. Take Nadia over there and stay until you think she feels comfortable. I'll be home about five-thirty or six." He scribbled his address on a memo sheet from Sheela's desk and told them the easiest route to take.

"Thank you," said By.

"I see why Sheela fell in love with you, dear," said Lillian. She turned to Sheela. "I'm sorry for being such a bear with you the last few days."

"I only wanted the best for you, Lillian."

"I know, dear."

Sheela hugged them both and sent them on their way before she turned back to Aaron. "You are absolutely wonderful!"

He grinned and bobbed his brows. "I know."

She took his face in her hands and kissed him. He stood quietly for a while, savoring her touch, then he circled her with his arms and kissed her.

After a long time he led her to the leather couch in his office and sat her down. "Sheela, I am going to say something that might upset you, but I must say it."

The grave tone of his voice alarmed her. "What?"

"I want you to invite your mother and your grandmother to the wedding."

"No!" She shook her head hard. "No!"

He lifted her hand to his lips and kissed her fingers. "Honey, they love you. They need you. You can help Bobby and Wade find Christ. You can help your grandmother grow spiritually."

"But I can't tolerate being around them!"

"With God's help you can."

She bit her lower lip. "Please don't ask this of me."

"Sweetheart, your past is in the past. Forgive your mother for your sake as well as hers."

"I can't, Aaron," she whispered hoarsely.

"Honey, you can. This root of bitterness has grown strong in you and it's causing all kinds of problems for you and for your mom and grandma. But God is greater than the root of bitterness. And His strength is in you." He gently wiped a tear off her cheek. "With His strength you can forgive Bobby. You can jerk out the bitterness by the roots so it won't trouble you further."

He made it sound so easy. "Aaron, you didn't have to suffer the beatings like I did." Sheela shuddered just thinking about it. "She doesn't deserve to be forgiven."

He pulled her close and kissed her closed eyes, the corners of her mouth, and her lips. He smelled the delicate aroma of her skin and tasted the saltiness of her tears. "If I could erase the agony you suffered I would, Sheela. But I can't. Only God can. But, honey, unless you willingly give up your anger and bitterness, He can't do anything."

She pushed her hair back from her face and looked pleadingly at him. "You're asking too much of me. She ruined my life and she does not deserve to be forgiven."

"That has nothing to do with it." He saw the look on her face. "It doesn't, Sheela. God doesn't look at a situation and say, Well, that's too terrible, too awful and I can't forgive it.' No. He forgives and He asks the same of us. God says to forgive and you must obey Him. For your own well-being as well as Bobby's. Unforgiveness brings grief, unhappiness, bitterness and can lead to physical problems for you."

"Oh, Aaron."

"Honey, remember God's nature and ability are in you. With His help you can forgive Bobby. And then you can get on with your life. You'll never be totally free until you forgive."

She leaned her forehead against his arm. "I don't know what to do."

"Yes, you do. As an act of your will, you forgive Bobby, and then the Lord will take care of the rest."

She pulled away from him. "Please don't force me to do this."

"I would never force you to do anything, Sheela." His eyes were sad as he looked at her. "I want to help you, but if you don't let me, I can't. It's the same with God. He gave you a free will to make choices. He'll help you if you let Him, if you don't, He can't.

"You make it sound so simple."

"It is simple, sweetheart, but it's not always easy."

"If I do forgive her, does that mean I have to go see her and be a daughter to her?"

"It's your choice. But you'll find, once you forgive her, you'll be able to see her without those old angry, hurt feelings getting in the way."

"Oh, Aaron."

"We'll pray together if you want."

"I want."

He bowed his head against hers. "Father God, thank you for my precious Sheela. She sees now that she must forgive Bobby. Thank you for your strength and love in her so that she can. As an act of her will she does forgive right now in Jesus' Name."

Sheela prayed silently as Aaron prayed. A tight band around her snapped and she knew that at last she was free of the terrible past. She knew even the scars were gone. She lifted her head. "Aaron, I am free," she whispered.

"Yes, sweetheart, you are." He held her close and kissed her until her world tipped and she knew only him. "Now, shall we agree on a Christmas wedding?"

She laughed breathlessly as she smoothed his hair with an unsteady hand. "How could we be ready so soon?"

"I have two sisters and a mother who will be glad to help."

The phone rang and she landed back on earth with a thud. She scooped up Aaron's white receiver. "Hello. Brooks Advertising."

"Sheela. It's Addie. Come quick. I need you."

"Addie?" Sheela reached out for Aaron's hand and clung to it.

"Hurry, Sheela!"

"Where are you, Addie?"

"In our lobby at the pay phone. Hurry!"

"I'll be right there," she said, but she was speaking over the dial tone. She turned to Aaron. "I must go to Addie."

"Shall I go with you?"

"No. This is something I must do alone. I should've done it when I first met them."

He nodded. "Run along then and take all the time you need."

She kissed him, grabbed her coat and purse and ran to the car, praying aloud for Addie as she drove. She parked in her spot and ran to the back door, unlocked it and slipped inside. Her heart raced and her stomach knotted as she ran to the lobby. It was empty.

Just then she heard a scream and she dashed up the stairs, shouting, "Addie! Addie, where are you?"

She followed the screams to Addie's apartment. The door stood open and Jill and Addie were inside, Jill holding a belt high to bring down on Addie who cowered on the floor.

"Stop!" cried Sheela. She caught Jill's arm and wrenched the belt from her hands.

Jill burst into tears.

Addie leaped up and clung to Sheela, sobbing.

Sheela sat on the couch with Addie on her lap. She watched Jill as she covered her face with her hands, her nails bright against her bleached blond curls.

"I knew this would happen," whispered Jill hoarsely. "Hey, I tried to stop myself. I tried so hard for so long. But today I lost my job and the rent is due and we have no groceries and Addie sassed me and broke my special cup. I couldn't stop myself this time." She dropped on her knees at the couch and gripped Addie's leg. "I am so sorry, Addie. Hey, I didn't mean to hurt you. Forgive me. Forgive me."

Addie cringed against Sheela and shook her head. "I won't. I won't!"

"Yes, Addie, you will," said Sheela firmly. She was talking to herself as much as she was to Addie. For the first time she could understand Bobby and the terrible stress she'd lived with. "You will forgive her!"

Addie looked at Sheela in surprise.

Jill's tears stopped and she stared at Sheela with her mouth open.

"And Jill, you're going to get help." Oh, why hadn't someone stepped in to help Bobby when she desperately needed it? "Together you're going to learn to deal with stress and you're going to learn to forgive." She told Jill to sit on the chair across from them and she talked to them with an authority that surprised her. "You're going to find a better paying job, Jill, and you're both going to move into a nicer apartment that won't depress you like this one does."

"But how?" asked Jill.

"I'm going to help you find a way. There is always a way. I'm so sorry that I wasn't able to help you sooner. But now I can. I can tell you about Jesus." And she did.

Later with the glow of one victory with her and before she lost her courage, Sheela drove to 1825 Apple Street and looked at the small house. Snow piled against scraggly bushes. Faded curtains hung at the windows. It looked just like the houses she'd lived in while she was growing up.

A strength that she knew came from God rose up

inside her and she walked to the door and knocked.

Wade opened it and stared as if he saw a ghost. Slowly he stepped aside. "Turn off the TV, Bobby. You got company."

Bobby glanced over and gasped. She clicked off the set and struggled to her feet. Magazines slithered to the floor at her feet. "Sheela. Is that really you come here to see me?"

Sheela stepped forward. "I had to come."

Bobby burst into tears. "It's a dream. I know I'll wake up and find out it's a dream."

"It's no dream," said Wade gruffly.

Sheela touched Bobby's arm. "I came to tell you that I do forgive you for what you did to me. I forgive you."

"You do?" Bobby's slight shoulders shook with her weeping. "Oh, baby!"

"I can't let the past ruin my life. Or yours."

"You forgive me." Bobby hung her head and sobbed harder. "I don't deserve it. But I'm so glad you do."

Sheela choked with emotion, but she managed to say, "I also want to invite you and Wade to my wedding. I'm going to call Grandma too."

Bobby used the sleeve of her sweater to wipe her face. "You want us to come to your wedding?"

"Yes."

"Oh, Sheela. Wade, do you hear that? She wants us to come to her wedding." Bobby reached out and gently stroked Sheela's cheek. "My baby's getting married."

Sheela hesitated, then opened her arms and wrapped them around Bobby. Bobby clung to her, sobbing and whispering her name over and over. Sheela pushed her cheek against Bobby's hair and wept.

Later Sheela walked into her office, her step light. She heard Aaron on the phone in his office and her heart skipped a beat. Smiling, she walked to the door and stood there, devouring him with her eyes.

He felt her presence and looked up, ending the conversation as quickly as possible. In a few lithe steps he reached her and took her in his arms. "I missed you. I love you!" His mouth covered hers in a kiss that left her weak.

After a long time she said, "How about a Christmas Eve wedding? That way we can spend our first Christmas together this year."

"I like it. We'll start right away to find a house. I saw one at the edge of town that I like and I think you will too. The yard is big enough for kids and it has three bedrooms."

"And since I want to continue working until we start a family how would you feel about hiring Jill as housekeeper and cook for us? She could find an apartment nearby and we'd be all set. She can finish high school and other training to help her launch a career. She won't have to worry about a baby-sitter for Addie."

"It sounds like you have their lives, your life and my life all in order."

"I do." She pushed her fingers into the thick, soft hair above his collar. "And I called Grandma about the wedding."

"You did!"

"And I went to visit Bobby."

"Oh, Sheela!" He hugged her tighter.

Her eyes glowed with triumph. "I can live at last!"

"We'll both live." His mouth touched hers and he said against her lips, "Together."

Her heart echoed the promise.